KU-692-219

Thanks so much, guys, for all your help. You know who you are.
M.M.

Published by Emain Publications Limited, 2014.

Author Mo Maher.

Cover design and illustrations by Gary Boyd.
Book design by Emain Publications & Big Rock Designs.

A CIP catalogue record for this book is available
from the British Library.
ISBN: 978-0-9573926-8-7

Printed by Nicholson Bass in Northern Ireland.

Also available in ebook on Amazon Kindle
ISBN: 978-0-9573926-6-3

Supported by the Creative Industries Innovation Fund

Russ On The Suss

Mo Maher

To Helen
love from
Mo Maher
(Maureen)

Chapter 1

Ned was after me. He was like the devil, his creepy little face popping up all over the place, staring out of shop windows, peering round hedges, following me.

I didn't know why.

Well maybe I did.

By the way, I'm Russ.

And that's another thing - I hate my name.

D'you know how many words rhyme with Russ? Bus, cuss, fuss, muss, puss, suss and, worst of all, wuss.

I asked my dad, why didn't you call me Dave? Brave, fave, rave, save, wave. Good words.

So why did I have to be Russ the wuss?

'Sorry,' he said. 'Actually we called you Russell and it's a lovely name.'

'Yeah, right,' I said. 'Bustle, hustle, muscle, tussle.'

Don't be a wuss,' he said, laughing.

That was the last time I heard him really laugh for a long time.
The trouble started with Dad going bananas one night.

Kelly, my sister was in her room pretending to do her homework.
Mum and Dad were in the kitchen.
It was quiet at first. Then Dad started shouting.

'Where is it?'

There was a banging sound like he was hitting the table. I'd never heard him like that before.

Mum said,'I don't know, John. I haven't seen it.'

She sounded scared which was scary in itself.

'You've put it somewhere, haven't you?'

Then he got really nasty.

'You know, dear, the way you put things in a safe place. Then we never see them again.'

She sounded like she was crying.

'Honestly, I didn't.'

'WELL, WHERE IS IT?'

He was roaring like someone crazy.

'Stop shouting. Please, John. The kids will hear you.'

'Well, it's going to be their problem too, isn't it?'

That's when I got really scared. A part of me knew what they were looking for, but I didn't want to think about it.

It made me think of Ned.

Ned wasn't just some mad evil creep. He was Susie's cousin. My friend Susie. And that was the problem. Susie would go crazy if I said anything about him. So I was stuck with him.

I went back up to my room and wandered round a bit, fiddling with things. After a while, I knocked on Kelly's door. That tells you how desperate I was.

'What?' She shouted over the noise of some weird music. I opened the door.

'What do you want?' she said. 'Can't you see I'm busy.'

'Yeah,' I said. 'Hard work, listening to music.'

'Actually I'm doing my homework.' She screwed up her nose. 'If you're going to insult me, you can go away.'

Are all sisters a pain? I only had one so I couldn't tell. Kelly was quite pretty, with short dark hair and big brown eyes. She always wanted to dress older than her age, which drove Mum nuts.

I was nearly twelve, two years older. Next morning Kelly and I were in the kitchen eating cereal. Mum was buttering toast. Dad was at the window looking out. No one was talking.

After a while, I couldn't stand it.

'What's wrong, Mum?'

She looked round and sort of smiled.

'What do you mean, darling?'

'Well, everyone's quiet.'

She looked over at Dad and made a face.

He made one back and said, 'Right, time for school.'

I got my school bag feeling kind of sick. Susie was at the school gates. We'd been friends for years, playing tennis, walking, talking. She was great-looking too, long blonde hair, blue eyes and a big friendly smile. She was the only person I could just be myself with.

'Hi,' I said.

'Hi, yourself.'

'Anything new?'

'Well, I got my hair cut, but you wouldn't notice that.'

'Actually I did. It's great.'

'You're a good liar, but thanks.'

That was the way it was with us. Real

stuff, jokey but kind.

At home, things got worse. They were searching the house. Dad was in GG's flat when he wasn't at work. No one went into the flat since GG died. Dad was over there emptying cupboards and drawers and banging things and swearing. Mum was doing the same thing in the main house. Well, not swearing, but saying things like,

'Where is it, where could it be?' and 'Heaven help us.'

'What are they doing?' I asked Kelly.

'What are you talking about?' she said yawning.

'You know, searching the house.'

'No, I don't know and what's more, I don't care. Why don't you just mind your own business?'

But I couldn't. I never could. That's what got me into all sorts of trouble.

I found Mum in the kitchen peeling potatoes.

'What have you lost, Mum?'

She whizzed round and raised her hands like a mad dancer.

'Russ, don't creep up on me like that. What do you mean?'

'Well, you and Dad seem to be looking

for something.'

She shoved a tea towel at me.

'Want a job?'

She was playing for time.

'Well are you?'

'Are we what? Oh, looking for something. No, why would you think that?'

'Well, you keep emptying drawers and cupboards.'

'Maybe it's your imagination,' she said.

I gave up. The search went on and on. Dad was angry all the time and Mum got sadder. Kelly didn't care.

And that brings me to GG.

My great-grandfather.

I can still see him, a big friendly man with a cloud of white hair and a matching beard like an Old Testament prophet.

He was a great man for puzzles. We did crosswords together and played board games. He had this wicked gleam in his sharp blue eyes. He said things like,

'Never listen to a woman...especially your mother.'

We were mates.

My parents had built a flat onto our house for him. He called it a grand-flat. I called in every day after school. We played Scrabble and Monopoly or card games. I beat him all the time.

He had a sitting room with a big brown leather sofa and a huge telly on the wall. The coffee table had a drawer you could put papers in. I used to hide my secret stuff there. The kitchen had shiny red cupboards with the washer and everything built in.

His garden was the best bit. The kitchen had sliding glass doors which opened onto the patio. GG had planted big tubs of red begonias which lasted for months during the summer.

'You have to dead-head them,' he said which sounded pretty nasty. The table and chairs were black with a yellow and green striped umbrella. We used to sit there chatting and playing cards.

A few weeks before he died, he said, 'Russ, I want to talk to you.'

He talked to me all the time, so I wasn't bothered. When he took my hand, I thought maybe it was a bit serious.

'If I go,' he said. Then he laughed. 'When I go, I'll leave you something, Russ. It will be your biggest challenge.'

'Don't go, GG.'

He just smiled and patted my arm. I didn't know what he meant. I couldn't even look forward to it because it meant he'd be dead.

I woke up one morning to find Mum sitting on the edge of my bed, still in her pyjamas. Her long brown hair was all straggly. She looked like she was trying not to cry.

'What's wrong, Mum?' I asked.

She took my hand. 'I have to tell you something very sad, Russ,' she said. 'Well, it's sad for us, but happy for him. GG has gone to heaven.'

It took me a while to work out what she meant. I knew that's how you talked about people who had died, but I couldn't believe GG had gone.

Then they spent months sorting out something called the estate. I asked Dad what it was.

'It's GG's things,' he said. 'What he left behind.'

'Oh. Why do you have to sort it out?'

'Well, he didn't leave a will, so it's a bit complicated.'

'What do you mean, Dad?'

He sat down beside me. 'Do you remember GG's pocket watch?' I nodded. Of course I did.

And then I was reliving it. GG was there talking to me. It was the night of my birthday, the one before he died. He told me how he got the watch. Its gold links jangled as he handed it to me. The cover had a picture of a horse rearing up with a small crown over it. I pressed the catch and it clicked open. The numbers were in big, black Roman figures.

'It was The War,' he said.

GG always called it The War. It was the Second World War; we learned about it in school.

'I was fighting in France. Times were bad. We were being pushed back by the Germans. Then I lost touch with my unit.'

GG had got lost in the French countryside. It had rained for three days. The fields were flooded and his uniform was soaking.

He arrived at a chateau – one of those grand French houses like a castle. The door was open and he saw a big hall with a huge fire place and old-fashioned paintings. He heard men shouting and crept down some stairs to the cellar. It was two German soldiers threatening a Frenchman who was begging for his life.

'I pulled out my gun,' he said, 'and moved to the foot of the stairs. My hand shook as I gripped the barrel.'

I was there with him, alone in a strange land, wanting to run away. But he had to save the Frenchman.

'Stop,' he shouted. 'Put your hands up.'

'I don't know', he said, 'whether they understood English but they saw the gun and raised their hands.'

He had to get the soldiers away from the Frenchman. He pretended there were others with him.

'Jim, Dave,' he shouted, 'come down here and watch these guys while I look around.'

He reckoned that would keep them for a few minutes. It would confuse them.

He had to set a trap, something to get them out of the house. The back door led to a patio which stretched along the length of the building. There was an empty swimming pool. It had a metal cover that could be closed over in the winter. There was a large button to work it. That's what gave him the idea.

'I was running out of time. I collected a small pile of stones and started to throw them into the empty pool. The first stone landed on the bottom with a loud crack. I waited for a moment and then sent a second. After that I threw the rest quickly one after another.

There was a commotion inside the house. Shouts in German and the pounding of feet. The two soldiers burst out of the kitchen door. I fired two shots into the air. They ran across the yard and jumped into the pool.'

'I ran towards the control for the pool cover and pressed the button. Fingers crossed. The cover slid across the pool. I could hear the shouts from under it. Then they started shooting. Small bumps came up in the metal. The men stopped firing when they realised the bullets were just bouncing back at them.'

'I ran back into the chateau and down the steps to the cellar. The owner was still lying on the floor, his hands covering his head.

"It's all right," I said, running over to him. "You're safe."

He looked up at me, terrified.

"OK," I said, raising my hands.

Then he smiled. "OK," he replied. "OK."

I helped him upstairs and we sat in the kitchen.

We could hear the Germans banging against the metal cover.

"Are they safe?" I asked.

"Yes," he said. "They will never get out."

'It was a relief when the banging stopped and an eerie quiet descended over the chateau gardens.

As it got dark, we could hear the sound of marching feet. We had no way of knowing which side they were on. My host beckoned.

'He led me up several flights of marble stairs. At the top was a heavy door. We could hear the soldiers getting nearer. He reached up to a shelf over the door and brought down a big iron key which he fitted into the lock. Behind the door was a set of narrow wooden stairs.

He locked the door behind us and we moved quickly up the stairs. At the top was a small tower room with a narrow window on each side. He motioned me to keep down and make no sound.

"I have a...how you say?"

He showed me a small round mirror which he held in turn over each of the windows. Through the east window along the road by which I had come, the remainder of my regiment was marching towards the chateau.

"They're ours," I said. "We're safe."

He clutched my arms.

"Thank you, my friend."

We made our way to the ground floor.

'After the men had eaten, I approached my host to say good-bye.

"My friend," he said. "You have saved my life. I want to give you the most precious object in my possession." He took a gold watch on a chain out of his pocket.

"This was given to my family by royalty. It is very valuable. Treasure it." He handed it to me and then kissed me on both cheeks.

'I placed the watch in my pocket. As we marched away, I could feel it banging against my leg. I slipped my hand down and held it close.'

I closed my eyes. I could still feel the pocket watch if I squeezed hard enough. So where could it be?

It was a bit of a shock to come back to the present. And to be kind of still in the past. Dad was saying. 'Well, it seems to have disappeared. He always said it was worth a lot of money. We can't settle his estate without finding it.'

Then, after a while they stopped looking and things sort of went back to normal.

I got used to GG being gone, but I still missed him. And I still didn't know what he had left me – what he called my biggest challenge.

So why were they doing it again - the searching thing? Why had Dad changed from a kind, funny man into an angry monster? And Mum just wasn't Mum any more. Was it something to do with money? Mum and Dad wouldn't tell me, but I had to talk to someone. Call me stupid, but I asked Kelly if she knew anything.

'What have you got ears for, brother dear?' she said. 'Of course it's about money. Dad's scared of losing his job. It's that thing called the credit crunch. I heard them talking about it.'

'Why didn't you tell me?'

I felt like stamping my foot and punching the wall, but she'd just laugh at me or tell Mum and Dad I'd been violent.

Chapter 2

Then we had the roof space thing. There was a folding ladder which stretched up to the wooden door set in the hall ceiling. Dad climbed the ladder, pulled down the hatch and climbed into the space above.

'What are you looking for?' I shouted up, thinking I might get some idea of what was going on.

'Not looking for anything, son. Just bringing down some stuff for Mum.'

Right, I thought. Believe that. Time to be creative.

'Dad,' I said, can I come up too?'

He gave me a funny look but said, 'Sure, if you like.' The roof space was like a big room, but the floor was rough and you had to watch not to hit your head on the roof beams.

There were piles of family junk in boxes and bags and plastic buckets.

'Dad, why do you keep all this stuff?'

He shook his head. 'If it was up to me,

I'd throw the lot out. It's your mother. She can't bear to part with anything.' We exchanged a man to man look and grinned. It was like the old days.

Dad poked about for a while, then said he was going down. I think he was a bit bothered with me there watching him. I said, 'Do you mind if I stay up here for a while?'

'Uh, OK,' he said. 'Give me a shout when you're ready.'

He went down the ladder and I looked around at my family's history. There must have been junk from the past twenty years. Maybe more if GG's things were there. I had a quick look in the boxes at the front. There was nothing interesting but it wasn't new stuff I was interested in.

Towards the end of the roof space the boxes got dustier. Some were too heavy to move and I climbed over them. When I got to the back against the wall, I saw five boxes which all looked the same like a set.

I opened the first one. There was a woolly thing on the top. I lifted it out and held it up to the light. It was GG's old grey pullover. I held it against me thinking about the times we had together. The next thing was his dark blue jacket, the one from his best suit. The trousers were underneath.

I emptied the box onto the floor. It was all GG's clothes. I wondered why Mum and Dad had kept them. Nobody would ever use them. I put them back and went to the next box.

It was full of books. GG loved his books. Some were old and battered. The first was the *Bible*, a big heavy book covered in black leather, with gold edges to the pages.

The next was his copy of Dickens' *Oliver Twist*. He used to read me bits of it.When I was younger I made my parents laugh shouting MORE at meal times. Then there was his copy of Shakespeare's plays. The rest were paper backs – *Pride and Prejudice*, *War and Peace*, *Wuthering Heights*...old and battered. I'll read them all, I thought.

The next box was full of sports stuff – a bowling ball, an old wooden tennis racquet, a few tennis balls and a baseball glove. I never knew GG was a sportsman. I wish I'd known when he was alive. I was trying not to cry.

The fourth box was things from his soldiering days. On the top was his old uniform. I opened out the jacket. Feeling a bit silly, I held it against me. Then I tried it on. The sleeves covered my hands and the bottom of the jacket nearly came down to my knees. I pulled up a sleeve and touched the sergeant's stripes on the pocket.

Then I looked down and saw the gun lying in the box. It was a Webley Mk VI revolver. GG had told me all about the different guns used in the war. I lifted it up and looked down the barrel. I knew it wasn't loaded. Once GG let me pretend to fire it, showing me how to aim and pull the trigger.

It all ended up with a click which was a bit sad when you were

expecting a bang. And suddenly I was a soldier, armed and ready for war.

I patted the pocket, but it was empty. Where was GG's watch? Why was it not in the box with the military stuff?

Then I remembered the last box. I had marched across the roof space playing soldiers.

I rushed back, climbing over anything that got in the way, banging my legs against the edges. The box was pretty small, sealed all over the top with Sellotape. I started to rip it off. Then I stopped, not knowing whether I should look in it. What if there was something really private?

I took the jacket off and put the other things back in the soldier's box. What could be in it that was so secret? It might be something important and Mum and Dad would never know if I didn't open it.

In the end curiosity won and I ripped off the pieces of tape. Then I opened the cardboard ends. It was nothing but papers. I lifted one out – an old bank statement dated November 1990. The next was a letter from the library saying a book was overdue.

I felt around the box under the papers to make sure the watch wasn't hidden. There was nothing there. I stuck the tape back on as well as I could. No point in looking for trouble. Then I shouted Dad and he held the ladder while I climbed down.

'Well, did you find anything?' he asked.

He was staring at me, his eyes narrowed like a hungry animal.

I shook my head. I didn't want to talk about the uniform and the gun. Then I thought of the books.

'Well,' I said, 'there was a box of books. I wouldn't mind having another look in it.'

'Right,' he said, 'will tomorrow do? Your Mum and I are in the middle of a serious discussion.'

'No problem,' I said, thinking, not again. 'Anyway, I have to do my homework.'

Dad went into the kitchen and I headed up the stairs as if going to my room. When they started talking, I crept back and hid in the hall outside the kitchen door.

The first thing I heard was Mum

saying, 'We couldn't really lose the house, could we?'

Dad was silent for a moment. Then he said, 'I don't think so. The honest answer is I'm not sure. The market is scarcely moving. Income is down. That makes the mortgage payments difficult.'

I didn't know what the market had to do with it. Sometimes we went to the farmers' market on Saturday mornings. They sold meat and vegetables. I had heard Mum and Dad talking about something called the credit crunch. It sounded like some sort of breakfast cereal, but it must have been really serious.

Maybe that was what he was talking about. Mum didn't say anything. Then Dad said, 'I thought Russ had found something, but it turned out to be a load of old books.'

I nearly missed what he said next. I mean I didn't really hear him saying it, but I remembered it later, like something recorded. It took time for my brain to catch up with it. I'm talking rubbish, but it was the shock of what they were talking about.

Dad said, 'If we could find GG's pocket

watch, all our problems would be solved.'

Then I heard them moving the chairs back and I crept up to my room.

When I was lying in bed later that night, I had a thought. What if there was something in the papers in the fifth box which might tell me what had happened to the watch? It was a far out chance, but it was worth trying anything. I loved our house. I didn't know before that I did, but the thought of losing it made me feel a bit sick.

When I got home the next day from school, the ladder to the roof space was still in place. I asked Mum if it was OK to go up and look at the box of books again.

'Yes, of course, Russ,' she said, looking all worried as if she wasn't really listening. She stood in the hall until I had climbed up.

I went straight to the fifth box. The tape I had put back loosely was off in a flash. Part of me was scared to explore the papers. What if there was nothing and we lost the house? Stop being a Russ, I said to myself. Get on with it.

I started at one end of the box and worked my way across. Most of the papers were boring. The bank statement I had pulled out was one of a set.

There was a collection of bills – electricity, telephone, credit card. There was a bunch of old letters which looked more interesting. Some were to GG's wife, my great-grandmother who had died about twenty years before GG.

I had seen old photos of her, a kind looking woman with grey hair and long, flowery dresses. The letters had been sent during the war and told funny and sad stories about his time in France. They all said how much he loved and missed her. The last one was about the French nobleman and the pocket watch.

The next lot were letters from the family and post cards sent from holidays. It was only when I was going through the last lot that I found an envelope addressed to me. It was just a plain white envelope. There were four letters -

RUSS

written on it in GG's handwriting. Underneath it said

Not to be opened before your tenth birthday

As I read the words I could see the old fountain pen that he carried in his breast pocket. It was my twelfth birthday in two weeks, so that was OK.

I nearly shouted out for Mum and Dad to tell them about it. Then I thought maybe that wasn't a good idea. What if it was meant to be a secret between me and GG? I held the envelope for a moment, then made myself tear it open. Inside was a single sheet of paper in GG's handwriting. It said:

On your ninth birthday

Dear Russ

I write this as I put my life behind me. As for the future, I want only your happiness. It takes much hard work and a great deal of courage to succeed, but it's a grand life if you can. Always listen to your mother.

To be lucky in life can only bring good. To be good in life can only bring luck.

Your loving great-grandfather
GG

I folded the paper and put it in my pocket. It was a weird letter. And the bit at the top about my ninth birthday didn't make any sense. If I wasn't to open it until I was ten, it couldn't be for my ninth. But GG was very old when he wrote it. Could he have been confused? I didn't think so. Dad always said he was sharp as a tack. There must be a reason for it, but I couldn't think what it was.

I couldn't think at all. My sister had her friend over and the noise levels were off the planet.

'Keep it down,' I shouted.

'Oh, shut up,' she shouted back in her ladylike way.

'Shut up, yourself. It was you making the noise.' She always brought me down to her level.

'Children.' Both our parents shouted at once.

I went into my room and closed the door to get a bit of peace. It was the one place on earth I felt truly happy. I wasn't allowed a computer in case I got into dodgy chat rooms. Not that I would have. But I had a TV. I watched the Simpsons and war programmes. I had to turn it off by nine on school nights, but I could watch later on weekends. I had a high bed with a desk under it. The floor was wood with a red rug in the middle. There was a section of the wall for sticking things on and I had posters of Man U and Star Wars.

I climbed up and lay on the bed looking at GG's letter. The way it was written was kind of serious and a bit old-fashioned. That wasn't like him.

Then I wondered...could he have...? Was it possible...? I told myself not to be silly. Just because I wanted there to be a secret message in the letter, didn't mean there was. Anyway, GG was sick and old when he wrote it. He wouldn't be thinking about puzzles.

But, what if...? I couldn't stop thinking about it.

I was still puzzling over the letter when Mum called me down for supper. Kelly's friend had gone home and the four of us sat down to pasta and chicken nuggets. Home-made, of course. We never had anything out of tins or packets.

Dad took me by surprise. 'Well, did you find anything interesting up there?

'Uh, not really.' I could feel myself going red. I hated telling lies, but I wasn't ready to talk about GG's letter.

It might be nothing. On the other hand, he could be trying to tell me something important. Luckily, no one seemed to notice.

My sister was yapping away about something silly and my
parents were giving her all their attention. She came in handy sometimes.

It wasn't until the next morning when I woke up that I got the idea.

It must have been my subconshus working during the night. GG had told me about someone called Sigmund Froyd who said that your mind can solve problems even when you're asleep.

I sat up in bed: NINE!

I remembered GG telling me about a book where someone had put in a strange number to tell the reader which words to choose.

Could he have done that in the letter? Could it be something to do with ninth words?

I grabbed the letter from under my pillow and climbed down to get a pencil.

When I underlined every ninth word, this is what it looked like:

Dear Russ

I write this as I put my life behind me. As for the future, I want only your happiness. It takes much hard work and a great deal of courage to succeed, but it's a grand life if you can. Always listen to your mother.

To be lucky in life can only bring good. To be good in life can only bring luck.

Your loving great-grandfather
GG

I wrote down the underlined words: behind, your, great, grand, mother, good, luck. If you put them in the same paragraphs, you'd get:

Behind your great grandmother
Good luck

It made no sense. I never knew my great-grandmother. She died long before I was born. I had seen photos of her in the old albums. Sometimes GG talked about her, said how he missed her. I didn't understand at the time. I only realised after he died how much you could miss someone. To know you would never see them again was terrible.

Behind your great grandmother

I tried to see her in my mind. The last photo of her showed an old lady with blue eyes and white curly hair. She looked kind. I thought I would have liked her.

I woke up the next day my brain bursting out of my head. Mr Froyd had helped me out again. I ran down the stairs in my pyjamas and stood before a painting in the hall. It was of a pretty woman about the same age as Mum. She had long blonde hair with a jewelled clip holding it back. Her shiny silk dress was the same shade of blue as her eyes. And that was it - it was the blue eyes which made me realise who she was.

I had forgotten the old picture of Nanny Mavis, GG's wife. It had been hanging in our hall since long before I was born, just one of those things that was there. I stood in front of it, almost afraid to look for the next clue. Maybe GG's letter was nothing more than what it seemed to be. As I reached up to pull the picture away from the wall, I heard Dad at the top of the stairs. I turned away and walked towards the kitchen.

'Hello,' he said. 'What are you doing down here in your pyjamas?'

'I was thirsty, Dad. I came down for a drink of water.' Oops, used that one twice. Have to think of something else for next time.

He glanced at his watch. 'It's time you were getting ready for school.'

And that was the end of that.

It wasn't until the next morning that I got another chance to look behind the picture. I got up early and this time there was no one to catch me. I crept down the stairs and tip-toed along the hall. I didn't waste time looking at the picture, but reached up and held the bottom of the frame away from the wall. I couldn't believe it. Sellotaped to the back of the painting was a folded piece of white paper.

I peeled off the tape and took the paper down carefully. Dad was moving around so I took it upstairs before opening it. Safe in my bedroom, I was so excited, I nearly tore the paper. What was it – the message? I opened it up. At the top he had written

Well done!

The rest of it was just a bunch of letters. It seemed to be in code. I couldn't make any sense of it.

RTXSLOZBPIRMJN

At the bottom he had written

Remember me

GG

Could I ever forget him? I hid the paper in a book and put it in the bottom drawer of my desk. Then I got ready for school and went down for breakfast.

Dad was sitting at the table with Kelly.

He gave me an odd look.

'Were you downstairs again this morning?'

'Just checking the time,' I said. 'My clock had stopped.'

I was getting good at lying and felt really bad about it. GG would have been disappointed in me.

Chapter 3

Susie was waiting for me on the corner. The brown uniform skirt and blazer looked good on her. Her straight blonde hair hung down in that style that looked messy, but was hard to do. I had seen Mum trying to do it with her straighteners.

'Hi.'

'Hi, yourself.'

We walked to school together most days. The others in our year teased us, but we were just friends. We were eleven years old, for heaven's sake - dating was the last thing in our heads.

She turned to me. 'Anything new?' It wasn't a serious question; she was just chatting. I hadn't told her about GG's message. I wasn't sure what to do. Then I decided.

'There is something,' I said. 'I haven't time to tell you about it now. Wait 'til after school. Give me ten minutes to pick up some stuff from the house and meet me at the end of the lane.'

'OK,' she said. 'See you then.'

I told Mum and Dad I was having a game of tennis with a mate in the park. I could have told them I was meeting Susie – they knew we were friends – but I'd have to listen to the usual stuff from my sister. *Russie has a girlfriend*. My parents weren't much better, hiding grins and looking away.

Susie looked at my tennis racquet and raised an eyebrow.

'Don't ask,' I said.

She shrugged. 'Well, what are you going to show me?'

I took out GG's letter and handed it to her. She read the original and then the hidden message.

'Do you know what it means?'

I nodded. 'We have a picture in the hall of my great-grandmother. She died before I was born.'

'And did you look?'

'I did.' I wiggled my hand like a magician and held out the paper. 'Da-dah.'

She looked at the message. 'And I suppose you know what it means?'

That was the awkward bit.

'No. I haven't managed to work it out yet.'

She studied the paper for a moment and shook her head.

'Why do you think your great-grandfather is sending you these messages?'

'Well, he's not actually sending them. They were already there.'

'You know what I mean.'

'I don't know,' I said. 'He must have wanted to tell me something. But I've no idea what.'

'What do your parents think about it?'

It was a good question but I didn't have a good answer.

'I haven't told them.'

She looked shocked.

'Why ever not?'

I did the confused guy thing, looking down at my feet and shuffling.

'I don't know.'

She looked disgusted. I didn't blame her.

'But wouldn't they want to know? I mean GG was your Dad's grandad, wasn't he? Wouldn't he want to know he had left messages?'

I had asked myself the same question.

The first thing was my parents' money problem. They had enough on their plate without worrying about weird messages from GG's grave. I couldn't tell Susie all that. It was family business. Personal stuff. I wanted to keep it to myself until I knew where it was leading. It was OK to share the mystery with Susie.

We spent some time trying to work out the code, but no luck. Susie asked if she could copy it down and take it home to think about it some more.

'You won't show it to anyone?' Not mentioning any names.

'Of course, I won't,' she promised.

'It's our secret.'

We arranged to meet the next day after school.

That night, after I finished my homework, I got out GG's paper. I was determined to solve the puzzle. What if Susie figured it out and I didn't? It wasn't that I didn't think girls were equal and all that, I just didn't want to be beaten by her. She might think I was stupid.

Now I knew that GG was leaving coded messages, I had something to work with. I looked down at the letters. They had to stand for something which would make sense. There were two possibles. Either the code was hidden somewhere or GG knew I would be able to figure it out. Who was I kidding? It was a bunch of letters that made no sense and my chances of figuring it out were zilch.

Come on, I said. Don't be negative. I decided to do some homework and give Mr Froyd a chance.

It was mostly maths problems so I had to concentrate. One was a horror and I walked around the room trying to figure it out. For a while I forgot about GG's puzzle. Even before I finished the homework, I could feel something niggling. I kept shutting it out, telling myself to finish one job before starting another. That's what my Dad always said.

And that's when I got it. It was like something exploding in my head: GG's sayings. You could always tell when one was coming.

We used to mouth them, saying them to ourselves before he did.

I didn't know what most of them meant but I knew them all off by heart. I just had to find the right one. First I wrote out GG's letters and the alphabet.

RTXSLOZBPIRMJN

ABCDEFGHIJKLMNOPQRSTUVWXYZ

Then I listed all the sayings I could think of:

Fools rush in where angels fear to tread.
A bird in the hand is worth two in the bush.
A stitch in time saves nine.
Neither a borrower nor a lender be.
No man is an island unto himself.
There are only twenty-four hours in a day.

I tried each saying against the alphabet. There are only twenty-six letters so the first two were too long. I started with the third:

I had to think about how to work it out. The first thing was to exchange the alphabet letters for GG's code. So I wrote down his letters:

RTXSLOZBPIRMJN

If I started with the *R*, that gave me an *S*. Then the *T* gave me an *I*.

The trouble was, when I got to X, the next letter, I had no letter from GG's saying to match it. The saying wasn't long enough.

So I needed to have a saying with 26 letters so it could match the alphabet. The only one of GG's with 26 letters was: No man is an island unto himself.

So I matched it against the alphabet and this is what I got:

Putting in GG's code

RTXSLOZBPIRMJN

gave me:

THEOLDFOUNTAIN

Even I could see that you could break it down into three words:

THE OLD FOUNTAIN.

Old fountain? Which old fountain? *GG, help me!*

There was no answer.

I met Susie the next day. She was late so we didn't have much time to talk on the way to school.

'Any luck?' I asked.

'Not really.' She looked a bit awkward.

'Don't worry,' I said. 'I think I've got it.'

'Look,' she said, 'we have to run. It's nearly nine.'

'See you later,' I said when we reached the gate.

The day went on forever. I kept

getting into trouble for not listening. Of course, the only thing I could think of was the old fountain. And suddenly Mr Froyd struck again. I knew what it was! I nearly jumped out of my seat.

'Something wrong, Russ?'

I came back to earth. Mrs Parker was glaring at me.

'Sorry, Miss.' I looked down at my desk and after a minute she went on with the lesson.

I had forgotten all about the fountain at home. I remembered Dad laughing about it once. He called it Mum's folly. She had wanted a fountain in the garden.

I had never seen it. I didn't even know where it was. Maybe it was in the middle of a flower bed or under some bushes that were so grown over, you couldn't get into them. There were lots of odd places in the garden where an old fountain could have been buried.

When the day finally ended, I met Susie in the playground.

'Well?' she asked.

'The old fountain,' I said.

'What?' She looked at me like I'd grown a horn.

'The message. That's what it said.'

'But what does it mean? Which fountain?'

I explained to her about Mum's folly.

'It must be still there, somewhere in the garden. Come home with me,' I said. 'We can look for it.'

Susie raised her eyes heavenwards.

'Have you ever heard of a wild goose chase?' she asked.

'You know that's another thing GG used to say,' I said. 'I'd forgotten about that one.'

She groaned.

'If you're not interested,' I said, 'you don't have to come.'

'Oh, I am. I'm just afraid it'll all lead to nothing.'

'Well, if it does, that's the way it is. I'll have to get over it.'

She smiled then.

'I really hope it leads to something, Russ.'

I got a funny feeling like when something in a movie makes you want to cry.

'Come on,' I said. 'Let's get on with it.'

When we got to the house, we went straight to the back garden. Mum waved at us through the kitchen window.

Susie put her school bag down.

'Well, where do we start?'

Good question. Could it be along the wall somewhere? I had seen pictures of fountains shaped like lions' heads with the water coming out of their mouths. There was nothing like that, but some parts of the wall were hard to get at where climbers grew against the bricks. Some parts down at the far end were crumbling.

'Let's try the wall first.'

'Why don't you ask your parents? They must know where it is.'

I couldn't think of a good reason. I just didn't want them to get curious.

'I want to do it myself. OK?'

She shrugged. 'Whatever.'

We walked along the wall, feeling the surface as if a fountain might be hiding there.

Susie kept shaking her head.

'I know you think this is silly,' I said, 'but bear with me. GG never did anything without a reason. I trust him.'

We searched all around the edges of the garden and found nothing. I was beginning to get hungry and Susie said she had to go home.

When I went into the house, Mum

asked me what we were doing in the garden.

'Were you looking for something?' she asked.

I had to think fast.

'Er, no,' I said. 'We're doing a project on walls at school. Susie just came to have a look at ours. I'm looking at hers tomorrow.'

'Oh.' She gave me a bit of a look, but she didn't say any more.

Phew, I thought. Then I had another thought.

'One of the things about walls,' I said, 'is that they have things built into them, like, I dunno, fountains and things. Do we have anything like that?

'Well,' she said. 'We used to have a fountain, but it isn't in the wall.' She gave me another look. 'You won't be interested in it then.'

She couldn't know, could she? Of course she couldn't. She must have thought I was just being weird.

'Well, I'd be sort of interested, apart from the project, I mean. I'd like to see it. Where is it?'

'Oh,' she said, 'it's got buried. I'll show you sometime where it used to be.

It doesn't work any more.' She stared out of the window, looking a bit sad. 'I used to love it.'

I couldn't say 'Show me now!' It was getting dark. I'd have to wait until tomorrow.

It was hard to sleep that night. Following GG's trail was taking over my life. And I still didn't know where it was leading.

The next day after school, I reminded Mum about the fountain.

'Can't it wait 'til the weekend?' she asked. She was peeling potatoes and the oven was heating.

'Oh, go on, Mum, it'll only take a minute.'

She put the last potato in the saucepan and filled it with water.

'Boys,' she said. 'Why can't they be more like girls?'

'Boring, you mean,' I said, grinning.

She opened the back door.

'Come on.'

She led me down the garden. We crossed the patio and walked across the lawn. At the far end beyond a patch of rose bushes, we entered an area which was a total mess. I didn't know why it had been neglected. Dad did the basic stuff in the garden, like weeding and mowing.

During the late spring he planted begonia bulbs in GG's big wooden tubs. They reminded me of him all summer. But the far end of the garden was like a jungle.

Mum stopped at the end of the tidy part. 'It was through here,' she said.

There was a fence covered with ivy on the side facing the house. On the other side it was all long grass and weeds. The small shed where Dad kept his tools was in one corner. The other corner was used for a compost heap. In the centre you could just see the top of what looked like a pile of concrete.

'It was there.' Mum was pointing at the concrete.

I walked over and touched the rough grey stone, rubbing my hand over it.

'What happened to it?' I asked.

She got the sad look again.

'It was a bad job from the start. The builder who put it in went bankrupt.' She saw me frowning.

'His business failed.' She shook her head.' The water system kept running underground when we were away on holidays. It wrecked this part of the garden. Somehow we never got round to fixing it. In the end, Dad put the fence up to hide it. We always meant to sort it out. There's not much chance of it now.'

'Why's that?' I wondered if she would tell me what they kept talking about when they thought I wasn't listening.

'Nothing for you to worry about,' she said. 'Well, you've seen it now. Are you satisfied?'

'Yeah, thanks, Mum. I'm sorry about your fountain. I'll fix it for you when I'm older.'

She gave me a hug. 'Come on and get your dinner.'

I had to wait until Saturday to get another look at the fountain. Mum went to the shops and Dad was on the computer. Kelly had gone to play at a friend's house.

I went down the garden and stood looking at the ruined fountain, wondering how I was going to get at it. I poked around the edge of the stone where it was stuck in the ground. I couldn't shift it. Maybe I could dig round it. I went back to the shed to look for a spade. It was locked. Usually it was open and I felt like kicking the door.

To get this far and be stopped by a stupid lock! I didn't want to ask Dad to unlock it. It would have led to all sorts of questions.

Time for my lock-picking skills to come into play. It was a trick I had told no one about. Sometimes on Saturdays I went into town with Mum when she was shopping. There was a book shop with a second-hand section. I liked to wander round it when she was in the supermarket.

One day I found an old book on solving household problems. There was a chapter called *Locked Out?* It told you everything you needed to know about opening locks. I had practised on a pile of old locks I found in a box in the shed.

I went back to the house to get my lock-picking kit and had it open in a flash. Piece o' cake as GG would say.
Dad wasn't very tidy. There was stuff piled all over the floor. I got the spade first and hacked away. It was no use. I got down about two inches, but the ground was too hard after that.

I needed something smaller. Back in the shed I found a trowel and a small hand fork. I tried both on the soil around the fountain. The fork worked best and I was nearly half way down when Dad appeared.

'What on earth are you doing?' he asked. He didn't notice that the shed was open. He must have forgotten that he'd locked it.

I heard myself saying, 'I'm trying to fix it for Mum.'

He didn't say anything. When I looked up he had a strange look on his face, sort of a mixture of amusement and annoyance. He scratched his head.

I frowned at him. 'What?'

'Do you not think,' he asked, 'that if it was easy, we would have done it already?'

'I suppose so.' I just wanted him to go away so I could get on with it. 'Do you mind if I keep trying?'

'Not at all,' he said, 'but you're wasting your time. However, it's your time to waste, so feel free.' He turned away and went back to the house.

I gave a big sigh, relieved that he'd gone, and went back to digging. As the last bit of soil was cleared away, I could see the shape of the fountain. It was a dolphin mounted on a stone base. The water would have come out of its mouth. I felt around it but couldn't find anything. I tried to get myself inside GG's head. I could hear him saying, *Think, boy, think.*

And I did. And thought what an idiot I was. The dolphin's head pointed upwards, its mouth open wide. I slipped my hand into it. The stone was rough and it scraped my skin. I pushed my hand down as far as it could go. Then I found it. A little tube stuck against the side of its throat. I had to get a knife from the kitchen to poke it out.

It was a clear plastic container about 5cm long. There was a piece of paper rolled up inside it. I pulled the top off and stuck my finger in to get the paper out. It was folded in half. When I unrolled it, there was a crossword drawn on it with clues written underneath.

RUSS ON THE SUSS

ACROSS

1. How many more without feeling? (6)
3. Were you in stitches? Sounds like it (2)
4. Not against? (4)
5. An endless fart? (3)
7. Beginning to doubt (2)
8. Could be better (4)
12. Had his chips? (3)
13. Prehistoric mammal. Spell it. (2)
14. An article heads south east (5)
16. What a snail delivers? (4)

DOWN

1. Love of tennis (7)
2. Container for a dumb ox? (3)
4. Does the poet put them before worth? (5)
6. In the midst of actors? (2)
9. Skater in the ditch? (6)
10. H-hail? (4)
11. Germany says no (4)
14. Some tool (3)
15. Scatter seed endlessly (2)

Chapter 4

Then there was a bit of a lull in my search for GG's holy grail, whatever it was. It was my twelfth birthday. My parents were planning a party and it seemed to take up everybody's time, mine included.

Personally, I thought I was getting a bit old for a kid's party, but I didn't want to hurt their feelings.

There was a big debate about who to invite. Dad wanted my whole class. Mum said I should just invite my friends. Dad said if you did that you were leaving people out. Mum said that was life. I thought it would be easier to invite the whole class because it's hard to choose between good mates and medium ones. And I didn't really want to leave anyone out. Anyway, Susie wasn't in my class and I wanted to invite her.

'What about Susie?' I asked.

Mum looked surprised.

'Well you can't really invite her to a

boy's party, can you?'

'I don't want a party if I can't invite her.'

Dad suggested I have the boys for the party and then ask Susie to come for dinner afterwards.

'OK,' I said.

It was all a bit over the top. For the next two weeks Mum made lists of food and drinks, games to play, invitations, goody bags, decorations. I kept telling her not to go to so much trouble but she wouldn't listen. This is your last kid's party, she said. Next year you'll be in high school.

Finally the day arrived. Balloons were hanging from the front gate. You could hear the music out on the street. I was a bit embarrassed by it all. But it was OK when everyone arrived. We played football on the lawn, musical chairs, pass the parcel. People bounced on the trampoline which Dad had hired for the day. It was kids stuff, but fun.

The food was terrific and everyone said it was a great party. There was one good thing I hadn't thought of. I got piles of presents – books, computer games, stuff like that.

Susie came for dinner and that was fun, too. I warned her not to say anything about GG's puzzles and she nodded and winked. It was our secret. Or so I thought.

Then Ned came. I couldn't believe he was in our house. Why was he there?

I heard him explaining to Mum and Dad. 'I've come to walk Susie home.'

'That's very good of you,' said Dad.

Susie gave me a hug before she left. Ned stood watching with a nasty grin on his face.

That night in my room I took out GG's crossword. I looked at the clues. My first thought was - GG, what were you thinking of? It was like an adult crossword, one of those in the Sunday Times that he used to do. I couldn't make head nor tail of it as he would say. I put my pyjamas on and went to the bathroom to clean my teeth.

When I came back I picked it up and tried to make a start on the clues. At second glance, a few were pretty obvious.

13 across - the old joke - Spell IT - was a GG favourite.

That gave me an I so I looked at 11 down. I read war stories all the time.

Germany says no couldn't be anything but NEIN.

Then 4 down jumped out at me. Poet and something before worth could only be WORDS as in Wordsworth.

That gave me a W for 4 across. GG used to say Those who aren't with us are against us, so I wrote WITH.

ACROSS

1. How many more without feeling? (6)
3. Were you in stitches? Sounds like it (2)
4. Not against? (4)
5. An endless fart? (3)
7. Beginning to doubt (2)
8. Could be better (4)
12. Had his chips? (3)
13. Prehistoric mammal. Spell it. (2)
14. An article heads south east (5)
16. What a snail delivers? (4)

DOWN

1. Love of tennis (7)
2. Container for a dumb ox? (3)
4. Does the poet put them before worth? (5)
6. In the midst of actors? (2)
9. Skater in the ditch? (6)
10. H-hail? (4)
11. Germany says no (4)
14. Some tool (3)
15. Scatter seed endlessly (2)

I'm telling this as if I got the answers really quickly. It wasn't like that at all. It took ages and then I fell asleep before I could get any further.

The next day Mum and Dad were clearing up after the party. I sat on the patio working on the clues and stopping to do jobs when they asked me. One time I had to carry stuff into the kitchen. When I came out, Susie's cousin Ned was there. He was wandering around the garden as if he was looking for something.

'Hi,' he said, when he saw me. 'I think I left my cap here.'

I hadn't noticed him wearing one, but didn't want to be rude.

'Have you found it?' I asked.

He shook his head. 'Nope. Must have been mistaken. Thanks,' he said to my parents.

'Sorry to have bothered you.'

Dad said, 'No bother,' and walked him to the gate.

They kept me busy for the rest of the day. When I remembered the crossword, I looked on the patio table. It wasn't there. I asked Mum and Dad whether they had seen it. I had to be careful. I didn't want to give anything away. But they said they hadn't seen a crossword. Dad told me it was time for bed as if I was using some delaying tactic.

The next day after school, I searched the garden and then the house for the crossword. I was sure I had left it on the patio table. Then I had a thought. Could Kelly have taken it? I could hear the TV in the living room. She was sprawled on the red sofa watching some kids' programme. Her pink jeans and navy t-shirt stood out against it and I looked at her as a person, not just my annoying sister, for the first time.

She looked older somehow. I remembered that she was the same age I had been when GG died. Maybe that made me more polite than usual.

'Kelly,' I said, 'can you spare a minute?'

She looked up at me and scowled. 'What do you want? I'm watching this.'

'I want to ask you about something.'

'Can't it wait? I don't interrupt your programmes.'

My new-found patience was running out. 'For heaven's sake,' I said. 'I only want to ask a question.'

She held her fingers up in a way that

looked pretty rude.

'Well ask it.'

It came out all wrong. 'I've lost a crossword.'

She started to laugh.

'Just answer the question,' I said, gritting my teeth.

'You haven't asked one.'

I was getting mad.

'Did you take a crossword off the patio table?'

'No I did not take a crossword off the patio table.' She said it in a sort of ner ner na ner ner kind of voice.

'What would I want a crossword for? You're really sad, you know.'

I thought she was probably telling the truth.

I left her and went into the kitchen. Mum was starting dinner. 'Doesn't Kelly have homework?' I asked. As I went upstairs, I could hear Mum giving off to her. Yes, I thought, clenching my fist. And then felt like a really mean person.

The next day after school, Susie walked home with me. I told her about the missing crossword.

'Oh,' she said.

It seemed a funny sort of an answer.

She didn't say any more.

'I don't know what's happened to it. It means I'm kinda stuck.'

'I shouldn't worry,' she said. 'I'm sure it'll turn up.'

When we got to our house, we went into the garden.

'Show me the fountain again,' she said. We walked up past the end of the lawn through the trellis arch. She bent down to it and touched the stone. 'It's beautiful,' she said. 'Why don't your parents get it fixed?'

'I don't know.' I didn't want to tell her about the money trouble.

We walked back through the garden and sat at the patio table. Mum brought us orange juice and biscuits. It was one of those happy, peaceful times, what GG used to call the calm before the storm.

After Susie left, Mum asked me to bring in the dishes. The wind had got up and the umbrella was flapping about. As I cleared the table, I noticed something fluttering on the ground underneath. I bent down and picked it up. It was GG's crossword.

The first thing I thought was, So that's where it was all the time.

Then I looked at it. It had been folded twice into quarters. I knew there had been only one fold when I took it out of the plastic container. Someone else had folded it again. I put it in my pocket and carried the dishes in.

Homework took up the rest of the evening. When it was finished, I was too tired to think about the crossword. I put it under the pillow when I went to bed and fell asleep knowing at least that it was safe.

I think Mr Froyd was trying to talk to me in the morning but I didn't want to listen. Questions like who knew about the crossword, who was there when it disappeared and who was there when it came back were not things I wanted to think about.

I met Susie on the way to school. She seemed to have a question in her eyes. I tried not to see it.

'I found the crossword.'

She clapped her hands. 'Brilliant. Where was it?'

'Under the patio table,' I said, thinking *as if you didn't know*. Then I felt terrible because I didn't want to think that at all.

'Have you solved it yet?' She sounded

really interested, as if she cared and was on my side. I couldn't make sense out of any of it.

'Not yet. I didn't have time last night. I had too much homework.'

'Oh,' she said. 'Well, let me know how you get on.'

I was determined to solve the puzzle that night, so I did my homework straight away. Mum asked me if I was OK. I think she was joking. I ate dinner, went up to my room and closed the door. Kelly knew I wanted to be left alone when I did that. Sometimes she came in anyway but that night she left me in peace.

I put GG's crossword on my desk. Time for a serious assault.

2 down looked like a possible. A dumb ox had to be some sort of play with words. I could already see it. The end of dumb = B.

Put it with ox and you get BOX which is a container.

16 across. What a snail delivers. I had taught GG about snail mail. So MAIL it was.

5 across. An endless fart – I liked that one.

GG and I used to make jokes about

farts when Mum wasn't listening. But I didn't know what the answer was.

1 down sort of stuck out. When you played tennis, love meant NOTHING. I knew that because Mum watched Wimbledon every year.

And it fitted with WITH if you know what I mean.

ACROSS

1. How many more without feeling? (6)
3. Were you in stitches? Sounds like it (2)
4. Not against? (4)
5. An endless fart? (3)
7. Beginning to doubt (2)
8. Could be better (4)
12. Had his chips? (3)
13. Prehistoric mammal. Spell it. (2)
14. An article heads south east (5)
16. What a snail delivers? (4)

DOWN

1. Love of tennis (7)
2. Container for a dumb ox? (3)
4. Does the poet put them before worth? (5)
6. In the midst of actors? (2)
9. Skater in the ditch? (6)
10. H-hail? (4)
11. Germany says no (4)
14. Some tool (3)
15. Scatter seed endlessly (2)

I looked at 1 across. How many more without feeling? How many could be a number, and that would fit, but what did it have to do with feeling?
Without feeling? Then I got it. Numb – without feeling. More without feeling must be more numb – that is NUMBER – pronounced 'nummer'.

12 across was another of GG's sayings. He's had his chips. Three letters. It could also mean he ATE and it fitted with NEIN. I wrote it down.

I went through the clues again to see if anything looked easier.

14 down caught my eye. I hadn't really looked at it before. Some tool! Three letters ending in A. I couldn't think of any tool like that.

Chapter 5

The next day, Susie's cousin, Ned, rang to ask whether I would like to go to the circus with them. It was an evening show so Susie and I couldn't go on our own. I wasn't sure about it. I didn't like Ned and I still thought he had something to do with the crossword disappearing.

But I didn't like to think that way about Susie. Maybe she hadn't done anything wrong. Maybe she discovered that Ned had taken the crossword and she brought it back. She wouldn't like to tell me that Ned had taken it.

I decided to go, thinking I might find something out.

The circus was on Friday night. I hadn't made any headway with the puzzle so I decided to forget it for the night and just enjoy myself. And I did. It was great. The clowns were really weird. Two of them only had one leg. They were tied together and walked like they were one person. Cool.

Next were the tigers. They sat on stools and waved their tails about while the trainer walked around them. Then he made them do things, cracking his whip. I found myself on the edge of my seat, holding on to the one in front.

But the elephants were the best. They did everything slowly. First they stood in a line, each one with his feet up on the one before him. Then they made a circle, each holding the tail of the next one with his trunk. Next they all put their trunks in the air and trumpeted. It wasn't that they did anything really clever. It was just that they seemed so solid and sure.

I wished I could be like that.

After the circus, Ned took us to a restaurant for a drink. He had tomato juice. Susie and I had Coke. I was never allowed anything with e-numbers. Mum said they made you hyper. I tried to tell her that you can't use hyper on its own; it has to go before something, but it still didn't get me Coke. I'm going on about this stuff because I still don't like to think about what started that night.

Susie started it. Ned had gone outside for a cigarette. She put her glass down slowly, twirling it in her hand.

'Russ, can I ask you something?'

'Course,' I said. 'Ask away.'

She looked me in the eye.

'You haven't solved the puzzles, the ones your great-grandfather left, have you?'

For some reason it was a worrying question.

'No, not all of them.' I looked down at the table and then back at her. 'Why are you asking?'

'I wondered,' she said, 'would you mind if I asked Ned about them? He could help you. He's older and he's very smart.'

I didn't want Ned to have anything to do with it. I didn't trust him. I still thought he'd stolen the crossword and Susie had brought it back. I trusted Susie. I knew she was just trying to help. I had to stop her from telling him any more. But I didn't want to hurt her feelings.

'I know you're trying to help,' I said. 'The thing is I really want to do it on my own. It's sort of a challenge. GG would have wanted me to do it that way.'

She nodded. Before she had a chance to say anything, Ned came back. I thought they exchanged a glance but I wasn't sure. We spent the rest of the time talking about the circus. Then Ned took us home, dropping me off first.

Mum and Dad were looking worried when I got back. They asked me about the circus and tried to look interested, but I knew they were thinking about something else. After a while, they said it was bedtime. I closed the living room door and made a noise going upstairs. Then I crept down again and stood outside the door listening.

Mum was saying, 'But how much do you really think it's worth?'

Dad said, 'It has to be thousands, maybe tens of thousands. I don't know how many. But look at its history. Given to him by a French nobleman who said it was the most valuable thing he possessed. It has to be worth a fortune.'

'But where could it be? We've looked everywhere.' She sounded really upset and I was a bit worried. Was I doing the right thing? But what else could I do? GG had left the messages for me. OK, I was afraid to think that this was what it was all about. But what else could it be? The pocket watch was missing. GG had left a trail. I still didn't know where it was going to lead. I decided I would figure out what the crossword meant at the weekend come hell or high water, as GG would say.

I met Susie at school. There was something different about her but I couldn't figure it out.

'Have you solved it?' she asked even before we said hello.

'Not yet,' I said. I hated feeling uncomfortable with her. 'I'm leaving it till the weekend.'

'Can I help?' She had an eager look like a tiger about to gobble up some small animal. It wasn't my Susie. I couldn't work out what had changed her.

'Sure,' I said, hoping I could find some way out of it.

'Tell you what,' she said, 'I'll come over on Friday evening and we can work on it.'

I didn't say anything.

'OK?' she asked.

'OK,' I said.

What else could I say?

I found Mum crying in the kitchen.

'What's wrong?' I asked.

'Oh, Russ.' She shook her head. Then she wiped her eyes and looked up.

'Nothing,' she said with a sad little smile. 'Just having one of those moments. Don't you cry over nothing sometimes?'

'Sure.' I hoped my smile was more convincing than hers.

Later I heard her talking to Dad. 'Russ caught me crying. I couldn't hide it. God, what are we going to do?'

I nearly told them about GG's messages. But I still didn't know where the trail would end. If it was something silly, one of his little jokes, they would be really disappointed. I decided to keep going on my own.

That evening I heard Dad on the phone. I didn't take any notice until I heard him say, 'OK, Ned.'

It was what GG called the cocktail effect. You could hear people talking but you wouldn't tune into what they were saying unless they said your own name or a name you were interested in. I wasn't interested in Ned, at least not in a friendly way. I didn't trust him and, to be honest, I was scared of him. So I waited to hear what Dad said next.

'That's very good of you, Ned. I'm sure Russ will be pleased.'

When he hung up, he turned around

and saw me standing there.

'Do you know who that was?' he asked.

'Ned?' I tried to look bored.

When he nodded, I said, 'What did he want?'

'You're a lucky boy.' He smiled. 'He wants to take you to the match.'

City and United were playing at Old Trafford. It was a game I'd love to go to. With anyone except Ned. I could see his creepy face with the hair falling over his eye and the beard, his skinny body in tight jeans and a tee shirt.

'I don't want to go with him.'

Dad stared as if I'd grown two heads. 'Why ever not?'

What could I say? I didn't trust him. I thought he was too interested in GG's clues. I couldn't explain all that to Dad.

'I just don't like him.'

Dad was frowning as if it was me that was wrong. 'He seems like a nice fellow to me,' he said. 'Anyone who offers to take a kid to a football game has to have something going for him. Anyway it would be rude to refuse.'

'You mean I have to go?' I couldn't believe they would make me go when I didn't want to.

'I think so, son.' He nodded.

I dreamt about GG that night. I was with him in France, helping to fight the Germans. When we had got them into the swimming pool, we went into the kitchen. The Frenchman had prepared supper. It was set out on the big wooden table, bacon and sausages with toast.

When we had finished, he put a record on one of those old-fashioned machines. It was trumpets playing, like a fanfare. Then he presented GG with the pocket watch. There were tears in his eyes. When I looked at GG, his eyes were watering too. They embraced each other and I clapped loudly.

The next thing I heard was Mum shouting that breakfast was ready. I lay in bed for a few minutes thinking. GG had never said where the trail was leading. It had crossed my mind that his pocket watch may be at the end of the search but I wasn't sure. If Mum and Dad hadn't mentioned it, I may never have thought that way at all.

Suddenly I was sure. GG was leading me to his pocket watch. I was sure of something else too. I would follow the trail wherever it led.

I met Susie at school the next day. She was friendly enough, but there was still something awkward between us.

'Hi,' she said. 'I hear you're going to the match with Ned. Aren't you the lucky one?'

I grunted.

'What?'

'Yeah,' I said.

'Well, you don't seem very pleased. That's a bit ungrateful, isn't it?'

'Look,' I said. 'I don't know Ned very well. And he's older than I am.'

'So? He's older than I am and I love going places with him.'

'He's your cousin. That's different.'

The bell went and we walked towards the door. 'Russ.' She was looking down, kicking at the ground.

'Yeah?'

'How's the puzzle thing going?'

I had to decide. Did I trust Susie or not? I never thought I'd ask myself that. I looked at her. Long fair hair, blue eyes looking a bit worried, caring smile. Same old Susie. I had to trust her.

'Still working on it. I have some ideas, but not there yet.'

'I could ask Ned. He's still willing to help.'

Trusting Susie was one thing, trusting Ned something different altogether. Anyway I didn't.

'Look,' I said, 'I want to work on it myself a bit longer. If I can't solve it, I'll ask Ned. OK?'

'OK.' She smiled and nodded. For some reason, she didn't look worried any more.

Ned picked me up for the match at two o'clock. I had put on jeans and a grey hoodie. Mum said I looked lovely.

I looked up to heaven. 'Mum, please. You won't say anything like that in front of Ned, will you? Or anyone else for that matter.'

She laughed. Dad called from the front door.

'Ned's here.'

I walked down the stairs and said hi. He was wearing cool trousers and a black leather jacket. His hair was slicked, his beard going down to a sharp point. He looked like the devil in one of those old paintings.

I didn't want to go but there wasn't much I could do about it.

A red MG was parked at the front.

'Wow,' I said. Last time he had been driving an old Ford.

He grinned. 'You like it?' He clicked the key and waved me to the passenger door. 'Get in.'

The seats were red leather, like the car. I couldn't believe how much softer they were than the ones in our estate. The match was brilliant. We won 2-1 in extra time. Ned took me to MacDonald's afterwards.

I tried not to think about what Mum would say. Junk food. It was really fun. The wooden tables and chairs were crowded with people talking and laughing and stuffing themselves with chips and burgers. There was a queue at the counter and I watched the staff filling the boxes while we waited. Ned asked me what I wanted. When I stood there looking blank, he said,

'Would you like me to order something?'

I nodded. 'Please.'

He got two chicken burgers with chips and Coke. I loved the little packets with salt and ketchup. I wanted to take them home, but Mum would have killed me.

I was munching the burger when Ned said,

'Well, how's the puzzle-solving going?' I gulped and started coughing. He pointed to the Coke and I took a swallow.

'What puzzle-solving?' I asked, wondering how he knew. Had Susie told him after promising not to?

He shook his head. 'You were telling me about it after your birthday party. Remember? You were trying to solve a code. You told me the letters.'

I didn't remember telling him, but I had the crossword on the table when he was there. I couldn't be sure it hadn't been mentioned.

'Well, did you find anything in the fountain?'

I was really shocked.

'How did you know?'

He laughed and smoothed his beard. 'I'm good at puzzles. You said your great-granddad used sayings all the time. It wasn't difficult to figure it out. The old fountain. Well, did you look in it?'

I didn't know what to say. If Susie had told him about the paper in the fountain, he would know I was lying if I said I hadn't.

I got an idea. 'Yeah, there was a paper, but I couldn't make any sense out of it and I threw it away.'

He looked really disappointed. 'Why didn't you show it to someone? I could have helped you with it.'

I shrugged. 'It was only a game. GG used to play them with me all the time.'

After that, he seemed in a hurry to leave and he dropped me at home without coming in to talk to Mum and Dad.

They were full of questions. I told them about the match, but didn't mention MacDonald's. No point in looking for trouble. The trouble was then I had to force another dinner down.

Chapter 6

The next day, Susie asked me how I'd got on with Ned.

'Fine,' I said. 'It was a good match.' I told her about MacDonald's and the extra dinner.

She laughed. 'That's what you get for not being honest.' She looked down at her feet and shuffled about a bit.

'Did Ned ask you about the puzzle?'

I had never kept anything from Susie. I hated the feeling of not knowing whether to trust her or not.

'Yeah,' I said.

'And?' She said it casually, but it wasn't really casual.

'I told him I hadn't solved it.'

'Oh.'

'Why?'

'Well, he might be able to help you with it.'

'I don't want anyone to help. I told you that. Anyway, I still can't figure out how he knows about it. I'm sure I didn't tell him.' I gave her a look.

I could swear she went a bit pink, but she just said, 'Well, we were talking about it while he was there. After your party, you know, when he came to pick me up.'

I nodded. There was no point in falling out with Susie.

'Russ, what's wrong?'

'What do you mean?'

'Well, you're different, unfriendly. Things aren't the same with us.'

I didn't like to say it was only different since her cousin starting hanging around. The bell went and we had to go into school.

That evening I was determined to finish the crossword. We had maths and English for homework which took ages, but I kept plugging away until it was done.

Then I took out the paper and smoothed the creases. I wondered how long it had taken GG to draw the lines and put the tiny numbers in the boxes. The in-between bits had been carefully shaded in black pen. I could see him working on it. Dad always said he was a perfectionist. When I looked at the perfect drawing, I could see what he meant.

So here goes I thought.

I went through the clues again.

3 across, a two-letter word ending in O, could only be DO, GO, HO, LO, NO, SO, TO or YO. The only one that had anything to do with stitches was SO. And that was it – sounds like SEW.

7 across looked the same. The beginning of doubt was do – so how about DO?

5 across – if you took the end off fart, you'd have an endless fart. Fart without the 't' – FAR. Brilliant!

That gave me an idea about some of the others. When we did crosswords together, GG sometimes said you had to take things literally. I didn't really know what he meant at the time, but it was like that ad – some paint that did exactly what it said on the tin. Like fart without the 't'.

So 6 down – In the midst of actors – was maybe just what was in the middle of the word 'actors'. How about TO?

8 across: G something, O something – Could be better. Well, if something was good, it could be better.

9 down. Skater in the ditch beginning with O? I hadn't a clue what that was.

I ran through the rest of the clues to see if anything stuck out.

15 down – Scatter seed endlessly? Sounded like another SO, sow without the last letter - its end. I wrote it down.

14 across – An article heads south east. The only articles I could think of were 'a' and 'the'. South east could be SE. That would fit. How about THE and SE? That would give THESE.

Mum knocked on my door. She was good that way. She never just barged in on me.

'Bed time, Russ,' she said. 'It's nearly nine o'clock. You were so quiet, I forgot about you.'

'I need five more minutes,' I told her. 'Just to finish this.' I had slid the crossword under my maths book.

'OK,' she said. 'Not a minute more.'

'Thanks, Mum.'

I really worked on 9 down. Skater in the ditch? Where would a skater be normally? On ice, I guess. So, if he wasn't on ice, where would he be? Then it came to me. Off ice. Which, when you put them together makes – OFFICE.

I was nearly there. 14 down. Some tool. Could be part of the word tool. And it began with a 't'. The problem was, it had to end in an 'a'. I looked again at 16 across. What a snail delivers? What else could it be but 'mail'. Then I remembered. GG always called it 'snail post'. It used to drive me nuts.

'No,' I would shout, 'SNAIL MAIL, GG. It rhymes.' I thought he was just old and stupid. Now I realised he was only teasing. I changed mail into post and 14 down became obvious. Some tool, or part of a tool, was TOO.

One left. 10 down. H-hail? What could it be? I tried everything I could think of. But it was no use. I nearly turned my brain inside out, but nothing came. In the end I had to give up and go to bed.

I woke at seven o'clock with my head spinning. GG used to say 'Hail and farewell', but he said it in Latin – 'Ave atque vale'. It came from a poem by some ancient Roman. So if 'hail' was 'ave', if you put an 'h' before it, you got 'have'. Thank you, Mr Froyd, I said, as I wrote the last word in the crossword.

It had taken hours but in the end I had got there. Then when I looked at the completed puzzle I realised I was no further ahead. What did it mean? There had to be a key.

Did I have to figure it out for myself? Or was there another set of clues somewhere?

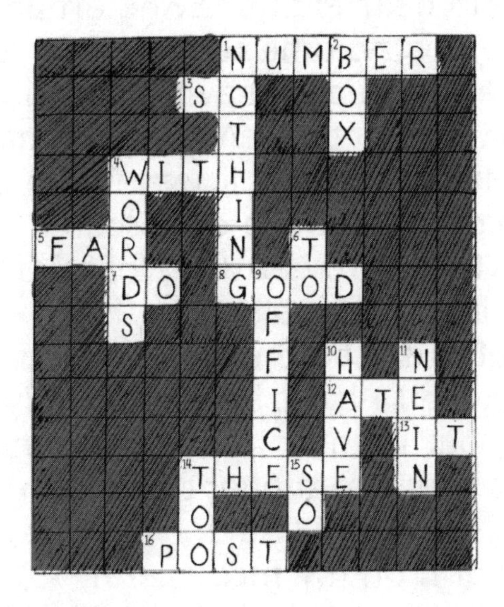

ACROSS

1. How many more without feeling? (6)
3. Were you in stitches? Sounds like it (2)
4. Not against? (4)
5. An endless fart? (3)
7. Beginning to doubt (2)
8. Could be better (4)
12. Had his chips? (3)
13. Prehistoric mammal. Spell it. (2)
14. An article heads south east (5)
16. What a snail delivers? (4)

DOWN

1. Love of tennis (7)
2. Container for a dumb ox? (3)
4. Does the poet put them before worth? (5)
6. In the midst of actors? (2)
9. Skater in the ditch? (6)
10. H-hail? (4)
11. Germany says no (4)
14. Some tool (3)
15. Scatter seed endlessly (2)

For the first time, I wasn't sure whether I was smart enough to solve the problem that GG had set for me. And I still didn't know what it was all about. I had a glimmer of a thought but I kept putting it away. It couldn't be.

I could hear Mum moving around so there was no time to look at it. She knocked on the door saying cheerily, 'OK, Russ, time to get up.' As if it was good news. Then I thought it was funny the way we didn't want to go to bed and then we didn't want to get up. What GG would call the human condition.

I met Susie on the way to school and decided to trust her completely. If I didn't, our friendship was over and I couldn't bear the thought of that.

'I've solved it,' I said. I could feel the big silly grin on my face.

'Great,' she said. 'Brilliant. Can I see it?'

'I haven't got it with me. I didn't want to take a chance on losing it. Come home with me and I'll show you.'

The sun was blinding. The umbrella was up over the patio table and the green-striped cushions out. I loved the summery look it gave to the garden. Mum gave us cranberry juice and home-made cookies. I ran up to my room to get the puzzle.

'Here,' I said to Susie, 'handing it to her. 'I've solved it but I haven't worked out what it means yet.'

'How do you know it's right then?'

'Well, it all fits. Look at it.'

She studied the completed puzzle for a few minutes and then looked up.

'Yeah, it looks right. How are you going to work out what it means?'

'I thought if I wrote all the words down, then see if there's a pattern.'

'OK, do that,' she said.

I wrote them according to their numbers, not bothering whether they were down or across. Here's what I got:

NUMBER SO WITH FAR DO GOOD ATE IT THESE POST NOTHINGBOX WORDS TO OFFICE HAVE NEIN TOO SO

Susie studied the words with a little frown on her face.

'What do you think?' she asked.

'Well, POST and OFFICE sort of jump out.'

She nodded.

'And BOX and NUMBER seem to go together. Isn't that something in the newspapers? You know like in those romance things – boy seeks lively girl for fun and maybe something more serious.'

I gave her a look. I wasn't going to admit to reading stuff like that.

'OK, what's left?' I wrote them down.

IT THESE NOTHING TO SO ATE NEIN TOO WITH WORDS SO GOOD DO FAR HAVE.

'There are two SOs,' I said. 'That reminds me of one of GG's sayings.' I looked again. 'Yep, there they are: FAR and GOOD. So far so good.'

Susie was impressed.

'That's really clever, Russ.' I tried to look modest.

'So that leaves us with:

IT THESE NOTHING TO ATE NEIN TOO WITH WORDS DO HAVE.'

We looked at each other.

'I haven't a clue.' Susie shook her head.

'Anyway, what's NEIN? That's German isn't it?'

'Yeah, it means no.'

'That's a big help.'

I grinned. 'Come on, we must be able to make some sort of sense of the rest. It's only a few words.'

'Hey,' she said, 'I've just had a thought. Doesn't the post office have those box number things? Post office box number – you know, for getting things delivered.'

I wasn't sure about it but nodded.

'You've maybe got something. How do they work? Do you know?'

'Not sure,' she said, 'but we could find out. Anyway, they have to have a number. Are you sure NEIN doesn't mean number nine?'

'Pretty sure,' I said. Then I thought about it. 'But it sounds like nine. Maybe that's enough.' I looked again at the list.'And what about ATE? That sounds like eight.'

'And TOO,' she said. 'Two. I think we've got it. Post office box number nine eight two.'

'How do you know that's the right order?'

Susie put her hand up to her mouth. 'I don't,' she said. 'How can we know?'

'What about the order they are in the crossword?' I looked down.

'NEIN is 11 down, ATE is 12 across and TOO is 14 down. So it could be nine eight two.'

'Hold on. How do we know ATE and TOO aren't just words? We'll have to figure out what the rest of it means.'

We looked at the words again. 'How about if we leave out ATE and TOO for now, see if we can make sense out of the rest of it?'

'OK, what have we got?'

I wrote down the remaining words:

IT THESE NOTHING TO WITH WORDS DO HAVE

'THESE and WORDS probably go together. If it starts with them, then a verb would come next. That's DO or HAVE.' I thought about it for a while, juggling them round in my head. Then I started to laugh.

'What?'

'That GG,' I said. 'Do you know what it is?

THESE WORDS HAVE NOTHING TO DO WITH IT.'

'What do you mean?'

'What I said. That's what the words say. It was GG's little joke.'

Then she got it. 'So we've solved it. Russ, that's brilliant.'

'Well, it is,' I said. 'But what next?'

'You go to the post office. Open the box. Duh.'

I wasn't sure it was all that simple. 'They might not let a kid do it.'

'Well, you can only ask.'

'That's true.'

Then Mum came in. 'Susie's Dad just called. It's getting late.'

I jumped up. 'I'll walk her home.'

On the way I thanked her. 'I would never have worked it out without you.'

'You'll let me know what's in it, won't you?'

I had a moment of worry. Then told myself I was being silly.

'Course,' I said.

Chapter 7

I didn't get a chance to go to the post office until the weekend.

I told Mum I was going for a walk with Susie. I should have asked her to go and then I wouldn't have to lie. But I hadn't thought about it. Well, to be honest, I didn't really want to. I still wasn't sure whether I wanted her to know everything, at least not until I had time to think about it.

Mum said, 'OK, see you.'

I had to think this out. I had gone to the post office with GG lots of times. The postmaster, Mr Watson, was an old friend of his. The two of them used to natter on about football, the weather, whatever was happening in the town. I had been in with Mum once or twice buying stamps, but he had just given me a smile and a wave. I missed the feeling of belonging I used to have with GG.

When I went in, there was a queue. I stood at the back watching the people and thinking about what I was going to say. When I finally got to the counter, Mr Watson said,

'Hello, Russ, what can I do for you?'

I forgot everything I had practised in my head and blurted out.

'It was GG, Mr Watson. He left a message for me, numbers, you know, for a post office box.'

'Ah,' he said. 'So you found it.' He smiled and nodded. 'He said you were a smart fellow. Have you got the numbers?'

I showed him the crossword and the numbers I had written underneath. 'Nine eight two,' I said. 'I hope that's the right order.'

'I'm sure it is.' He took the paper and told me to wait a minute. When he came back, he was carrying a brown envelope. It had my name on it written in GG's handwriting.

'Here you are, Russ. Just sign here, will you.'

I wrote my name on the form and he handed me the envelope.

'Good luck,' he said.

'Thanks, Mr Watson.'

As I left the post office, I met Susie's cousin Ned.

'Hello, Russ,' he said with a little laugh. His beard seemed to quiver like a rat's whiskers. 'Fancy meeting you here.' He looked surprised, but I had the feeling that he expected me to be there. Could he have followed me? GG used to call it paranoya, thinking people were following you or talking about you.

'Oh, Hi, Ned.' I tried to walk past him, but he managed to block me without seeming to. I noticed then that he was staring at the envelope. I tried to hold it so he couldn't see the writing. Would he have recognised GG's writing? I didn't know but I wasn't going to take a chance.

'Well, what are you up to man?'

'Oh, just picking something up for my Dad.' I mumbled the words, hoping he wouldn't sense I was lying.

'Did you ever sort out the GG thing? Susie won't tell me what's going on. She says it's a secret.' He was still trying to look at the envelope.

'Ned, sorry, I'm in a bit of a hurry. My Dad's waiting for this.'

'OK, man, no problem. See you.' He gave me a wave and walked up the road. When I was walking home I kept looking round expecting him to be following. The guy was driving me nuts.

When I got home, Mum asked how Susie was. I had forgotten she was my excuse for going out. I caught myself just in time.

'She's fine,' I said. 'Says hello.'

She gave me a funny look. 'What have you got there?' she asked.

'Uh, nothing.' I must be the worst liar in the world. I tried to screw up the envelope pretending it was rubbish. Luckily, Kelly shouted 'Mum' and took her mind off it.

'OK, coming,' she said.

I went up to my room and closed the door. Everything told me this was the moment. My head was crowded with GG sayings. All would be revealed. The die was cast. There was a new dawn.

I sat on the bed and tore open the envelope. Then I closed my eyes and breathed in hard. Please, I thought, let this be it. Let it be the end of the search. I looked up to heaven. Are you listening, GG? When I looked down, there was a folded piece of paper.

As I opened the paper, my hands were shaking so much I dropped it on the bed. Come on, man, I said to myself and grabbed the paper, spreading it out on the pillow. And sat there looking at - I didn't know what. It was a picture. Well it looked like a picture. There was a hook like you hang clothes on and there was something hanging on it. It looked like one of those furry things women used to wear in the old days, stoles I think you call them.

So, what was GG telling me? I hadn't a clue. Something to do with stealing? Or sheep? Or hooks? Or something I was too stupid to figure out?

Time to give it a rest, let Mr Froyd have a go. I tried to put it out of my head. It was a pretty good weekend. Kelly was out with her friends most of the time. Mum and Dad seemed a bit calmer. Maybe they were doing the same as me. Don't think about it - it will all work out.

Yeah, I know, call me an idiot.

Of course I couldn't stop thinking about it. A stole on a hook. If it was a woman's thing, would a woman be able to help? And which woman? I didn't think Susie would know about furry stoles. And she'd probably just laugh at me.
And then tell Ned.

What about Mum? I didn't want to get

her involved, but maybe there was a way of doing it without her knowing.

I went down to the kitchen. She was putting a tray of vegetables in the oven.

'Mum,' I said.

She gave a bit of a jump and banged the pan against the rack. Not the best way to start.

'Sorry, I didn't mean to give you a fright.'

She closed the oven door and turned round. 'It's OK, Russ, I didn't hear you come in. What is it?'

'Oh, it's just some silly competition. We have to say what we think something means. I just wondered what you would think.' I showed her the picture.

She looked at it, then frowned. 'Yuk,' she said.

'What?' I couldn't see what was bothering her.

'It looks like a tail, you know, a sheep's tail.'

'Oh.'

Which wasn't a lot of help.

'Er, thanks, Mum.'

I took it back and went up to my room. A sheep's tail hanging on a hook. Mr Froyd was going nuts; I could feel him whizzing around in my head. Tail, Russ, tail. Tale.

Hanging.

Then I got it. Thereby hangs a tale. One of GG's favourite sayings. So, if Mr Froyd was right, it had something to do with a tale, in other words, a story.

OK, but that didn't get me very far. What story?

What stories did we have together? I couldn't think of any. Which was strange. GG was a great reader and I liked reading. But I couldn't think of any books we'd talked about. Except maybe Harry Potter. I had just started to read him before GG went to heaven. Was there anything in the series that might help? I didn't think so. GG had never read them.

He only knew about them because I told him what I was reading.

The only other stories I could think of were the books in the roof space. But they were just books – some old classics and stuff. What could they tell me? There was only one answer. I had to look at them again. Which brought another problem. How to get back in the roof space without making Dad suspicious?

Only one way to find out.

I went downstairs. Mum was still in the kitchen.

'Where's Dad?' I asked, trying to sound casual.

'Why?' she answered, frowning.

It looked like back to normal or what had become normal. Why would a mum ask why you wanted to know where your dad was?

Caught by surprise, I just blurted it out. 'I wanted to ask him if I could go into the roof space.'

She frowned again. 'I don't think that's such a good idea,' she said.

'Uh, why not, Mum?'

She took a deep breath which sounded a bit shaky to me.

'He's….' She stopped. 'Nothing. Just… it's dinner time.'

'Oh, right. OK. Well, where is he?' If it was dinner time, why wasn't he there?

'He's just doing some stuff in his study. But I wouldn't bother him if I were you.'

'OK.'

That looked like the end of that. For today anyway.

Dad came into the kitchen.' Dinner

ready?' he asked. 'I've more work to do.'

Mum looked a bit offended. 'Yes, sir,' she said.

He laughed then and said, 'Sorry.'

Mum called Kelly and we sat down to eat.

Dad seemed OK, so I took a chance.

'Dad, you know GG's books in the roof space?'

He nodded.

'Do you think I could have another look at them? I'd like to start reading them.'

'Sure,' he said. 'Would tomorrow do? I'm a bit tied up tonight.'

'Yeah, that'd be fine.' I was pretty disappointed, but at least he hadn't said no.

The next day was Sunday. Everyone slept late except me. I was up at eight waiting to get into the roof space. Dad didn't appear until ten and then we all had to have breakfast. It was nearly lunch time before I could ask him to open it up.

He groaned. 'Couldn't it wait, Russ? Until tomorrow?'

'Sorry, Dad. Please. It's school tomorrow and you'll be at work. Go on, Dad, it'll only take a minute.'

Please, please, I thought, fingers crossed.

'Oh, OK,' he said. 'Let's get it over with.'

He pulled the ladder down and climbed up to push the door open. 'Want any help?' he asked.

'No thanks, Dad. I just want to look at the books.'

'OK, son.' He came down.

I ran up the steps and just missed banging my head on the edge.

'Careful,' Dad said. I thought he was going to stay and watch me, but he went into the living room.

I rushed over to the box of books and pulled it open. Then I stopped. What if I was wrong about the picture? It was a heck of a jump from a furry thing on a hook to stories in books. Get on with it, man. Either it is or it isn't. I dived into the box and pulled out the books. They were no different from what I remembered - the *Bible, Oliver Twist*, Shakespeare, *War and Peace*, *Wuthering Heights*. What could they tell me? I couldn't think of anything.

I sat on the floor. For the first time I felt like giving up. Mad with frustration, I kicked the box so hard it fell over. And then sat there stunned. There was another box underneath. Oh, GG.

I ripped the top off and saw two piles of books, paperbacks that looked new, nothing like the battered old copies of the classics that I remembered. I lifted them out and put them on the floor. There were seven. I looked at the titles:

The Lion, the Witch and the Wardrobe
Little House on the Prairie
Peter Pan
Swallows and Amazons
Watership Down
The King of the Golden River
The Serpent's Children

I knew some of them – *Little House on the Prairie*, *Peter Pan*, *Watership Down*. I'd only read *Peter Pan*. I seemed to remember GG talking about *The Lion, the Witch and the Wardrobe*.

But that didn't really tell me anything. If they were meant to be a clue telling me what to do next, I hadn't a clue how to work it out. Did I have to read them? Maybe. But that didn't really fit in with the clues so far.

I put the books in a row in the same

order they were in the box. In case the order was important. But nothing stuck out. I thought I'd better have another look at GG's first clue in case I was missing something.

I crept down the ladder hoping to sneak to my room and get the picture. As soon as I got to the ground, Dad came out of the living room.

'Finished?' he asked.

'Not yet, Dad. Just want to go to the toilet.'

He grunted and went back.

I had to go through all the motions, if you get me, flush the toilet and wash my hands. I sneaked into my bedroom and grabbed the picture. Crept back up to the roof space before Dad could catch me.

The picture looked the same as I remembered. A hairy looking tale hanging on a hook. The only thing I hadn't noticed before was a little sign above the hook. It was the number one in black on a round white disc. Did it mean anything? I thought about it. Number one. The first book? That was *The Lion, the Witch and the Wardrobe*. No help there. Or if there was, I didn't know what it might be.

Number one. What did it mean? If not

first book, what other firsts were there? Mr Froyd, where are you? Well, there was the first word. I worked that out for myself. I looked through each book and wrote down the first word.

I got Once, A, Roger, In, The, All, Two.

I jiggled them round in my head but whatever order I put them in, it didn't make any sense.

What next? The authors' names? C S Lewis, Laura Ingalls Wilder, J M Barrie, Arthur Ransome, Richard Adams, John Ruskin and Lawrence Yep. First names? That gave me C S (I didn't know what it stood for), Laura, J M (same problem), Arthur, Richard, John, Lawrence. No better.

Then Mr Froyd struck like a knife through my brain. How about first letters, idiot? I wrote down the first letters of each book title: T, L, P, S, W, T, T. Shifted them round. Couldn't make anything out of them. Did three Ts mean something? Couldn't think of anything.

Start again. I picked up *The Lion, the Witch and the Wardrobe*. Author C S Lewis, surname beginning with L. The next one, Ingalls Wilder, gave me an I. Quickly I wrote down the rest of them.

B, R, A, R, Y.
Put L I in front and what do you get?
LIBRARY! I couldn't believe it.

That was it! It had to be. I mean, it was all about books and it led to the library. What else?

I wanted to go straight to the library, but couldn't because it was Sunday. What a pain. I usually went on Saturdays, but that was nearly a week away and I couldn't wait that long.

Then Susie called over and I was so wired up I told her all about it.

'Wow,' she said. 'that was really smart of you, Russ. I don't think anyone else could have figured it out.'

I wanted to beat my chest and howl but I just shrugged and said, 'Thanks, Susie, it's only because I knew GG so well. Anyway, I still have to find out what comes next. I don't suppose the library will be the end of the trail.'

'No,' she said, 'when are you planning to go?'

I wished she wouldn't ask me things like that. I knew she was only interested, but it made me think of Ned. Ok, I knew it was nutty of me, but that's the way it was.

'Not sure yet,' I said. I might have to wait 'til Saturday.'

She nodded. 'Well let me know. Maybe I could go with you?'

'Sure,' I said. 'That would be good.'

She gave me a look and I felt guilty. How did girls always know when you were fudging?

She stayed a bit longer and we talked about nothing, then I walked her home.

'I'll let you know,' I said, 'when I'm going.'

She nodded and said, 'Night, Russ.'

Next morning at breakfast, I said casually, 'I might call in at the library after school.'

Mum, Dad and Kelly looked at me.

'What?' I said.

Mum laughed. 'It sounded as if you were making an important announcement.'

Great, I thought, so much for casual.

'Sorry,' I said, then thought, why am I saying sorry?

Start again. 'What's wrong with you all? I said I was going to the library. Is that some big deal?

Kelly looked up to heaven. 'So why are you telling us, brother dear? You must think it's a big deal.'

I felt like kicking the table. I'd never think of kicking Kelly, would I?

'What are you going for, Russ?' Mum was trying to look interested.

'A book,' I said and they all laughed. Which was fair enough, I suppose.

'And what book would that be?' Kelly had that nasty smug look on her face.

And my mind went blank.

'Er...none of your business, Miss Nosy Parker,' I said, half-ashamed but relieved I'd found any sort of an answer.

They all looked at me again.

'Something you shouldn't be reading maybe?' Kelly said it in her silly ner ner voice.

'You are such a pain.' The words were out before I could stop them.

'RUSS!' Mum and Dad shouted at the same time.

'Sorry,' I muttered, but I wasn't really. 'Look,' I said, trying to sound reasonable, 'I said I was going to the library just so you wouldn't be worried when I was late home. Is there something wrong with that?'

'No, of course not.' Mum was trying to sound reasonable now. 'But you did manage to turn it into something.'

I got up from the table. 'OK, gotta go. See you later.'

I grabbed my school bag and ran before they could start again.

It was a long day. Then I had to avoid Susie so she wouldn't know I was going to the library. Which made me feel worse. I got away as soon as the bell went and ran up Main Street. The library was on Dawson Street. Once I got round the corner, I was safe. I slowed down and looked in shop windows, not really looking, just thinking about what I might find and how I would find it.

The library was an old grey building with wide steps leading up to big glass doors. I went in and stood there not having a clue where to go next. Where would I find GG's message? Maybe I could feel under all the shelves to see if there was anything stuck there.

But that didn't make sense. They had to take out the books and clean the shelves. Anyway, someone might find it by accident. GG wouldn't take a chance on that. So I had to ask someone. The obvious person was Mr Stewart, the librarian. It was like the Post Office all over. Sort of. It seemed kind of normal for the Post Office to keep letters for people. It wasn't like that in the library. But I couldn't think of anything else. Mr Stewart was busy at the desk checking out someone's books. I hung back, waiting until he was finished.

Mrs Elliott was at the other desk.

'Can I help you?' she asked.

'Uh, sorry,' I said, 'I want to talk to Mr Stewart.'

She looked a bit offended. I smiled and said, 'Thanks' but she didn't look any happier.

When Mr Stewart was free, I went up to him.

'Hi, Russ,' he said, 'how are you?'

'Fine, thanks, Mr Stewart.'

We stood there looking at each other.

'Well,' he said, 'what can I do for you?'

He had a look about him like he was waiting for something. Could it be?

I said, 'GG, you know, my great-grandfather...' I didn't know what to say next.

He nodded. 'Tell me,' he said, 'what's on your mind.'

I thought, what the heck. 'GG left me a message. I think it might be at the library, but I don't know any more than that.'

He smiled. 'I thought you'd never ask.'

'You mean...?' I said.

'Yes, I've been saving it for you. Wait there a minute and I'll get it.'

I was shaking. Please let this one tell me what's going on. Please, GG.

Mr Stewart came back with an envelope.' Here you are, Russ. Good luck with your adventure. GG loved you very much.'

I took the envelope. 'Thanks, Mr Stewart. I'll let you know what happens.'

I tried not to run to the glass doors, but did a sort of fast walk which must have looked even sillier. I went through the door and turned to wave at Mr Stewart. And stopped in my tracks.

He and Ned were standing with their heads together. Mr Stewart was nodding and talking and pointing to something on his desk.

Ned nodded back and then he laughed, his horrid sharp teeth sticking out. I couldn't believe Mr Stewart would do that to me. Then Ned looked over and saw me. He put a hand up to Mr Stewart, said something and started walking towards the door. I ran then and didn't stop 'til I got home. I was panting when I went through the door.

Of course, just my luck, Kelly was in the hall.

'Somebody chasing you?' she asked. 'They must be hard up for company.'

I ignored her and ran up the stairs to my room.

I sat on the bed and tried to slow down my breathing. Take deep breaths and count up to ten. I could hear GG saying it. I held the envelope tight against my chest while I counted, then forced myself to open it.

I closed my eyes and took out what felt like a card. When I looked, there was nothing on the side facing me. Just a white card. Oh, GG, don't let it be blank. I turned it over. There were two words written on it in big black capitals.

MAXIMUM SAFETY

Right, I thought, make sense of that. And here we go again.

And thanks, GG, a blank card would have told me as much.

Hold on, I thought. Just because you

don't get it right away doesn't mean it can't be figured out.

But it wasn't telling me anything. It was just like GG telling me to be careful. Which didn't make sense either. If I'd been careful, I wouldn't have got this far. Of course, he didn't know about Ned. But why would he wait 'til now to tell me to be careful. Unless the next bit was going to be more dangerous.

MAXIMUM SAFETY

If he was telling me to be as safe as possible, I mean, if that's all it meant, then he wasn't giving me any clues about where to go next. So it must mean more than that. So maybe where I was supposed to go was a place of maximum safety?

I tried to think of places you could call that. Well, there was church. GG wasn't much of a church man even though he was a real Christian and read the *Bible*. I didn't think he'd leave a clue in a church. Police station? No, that wasn't a runner as he would say. You can't mess about with police stations.

I couldn't think of anywhere else.

Except the obvious. The safest place for everyone. Home? But if that was what he meant, I still had the same problem. No clue. Just home. It wasn't enough. So I was missing something.

Maybe, if home was the answer, and I thought it had to be, I should start looking around the house. Whatever I was looking for must be well hidden because no one had found it.

Then I had another thought. Home to GG was his flat. If it was there, it would make it a whole lot easier. First I could search the flat in private and second it was much smaller than the house, so there wouldn't be too many places to look.

But, of course, nothing is that simple. It was Monday evening; first there was dinner, then homework. I couldn't just go to GG's flat without giving a reason. And I couldn't think of anything. I decided to leave it 'til the weekend. It was hard, but it would give me a better chance.

The week crawled. I kept thinking about the clue

MAXIMUM SAFETY

but even Mr Froyd seemed to have given

up. Saturday finally came and I had to find an excuse.

'Mum,' I said after breakfast, 'do you think I could spend a bit of time in GG's flat?'

'What for?' she shot back, a suspicious look on her face.

'Er, nothing really,' I said. 'Just wanted to be near him for a while.'

'Oh, sorry, Russ. You took me by surprise. Yes, of course, you can. I'll open it up for you.'

'Thanks, Mum.'

We went down the hall to GG's flat and she unlocked the door. 'OK?' she asked.

I nodded. 'Fine thanks, Mum.'

I was afraid she was going to follow me in, but thank heaven she went away. When I went in, I was shocked. Not because it was different from how I remembered it, but because it was the same. I expected GG to come out of the kitchen the way he used to and offer me ginger nuts or ice cream or maybe a Mars bar.

'Don't tell your Mum,' he would say, putting his finger to his lips. I stood there for a minute, just missing him. I could feel tears in my eyes. Come on, you big wuss, I said to myself. GG wouldn't want you to behave like this.

I closed the door and stood there, wondering where to start. I didn't know what I was looking for, so it was hard to know where to look. I started looking in cupboards.

Nothing. I even felt under the shelves in case something was stuck there. I didn't find anything. No great surprise. I checked every drawer in the flat. Same result.

What next? If there was anything there, it had to be hidden.

MAXIMUM SAFETY.

So it had to be safe.

Safe.

Safe?

SAFE!!!

What had taken me so long? Where were you, Mr Froyd? It was so obvious. Anyway, no point in moaning about it. Just get on with it. I started working my way around the walls. Well, that's where safes were, wasn't it? Except there wasn't a safe in sight. OK, GG, were did you hide the safe?

It had to be behind something. Duh. But I couldn't see anything that could have a safe stuck behind it. The wardrobes and all the kitchen units were built in. I looked behind the moveable furniture like bedside tables and chests of drawers. Nothing. The bathroom had a cabinet stuck on the wall. I gave it a shove and, believe it or not, it moved. No, I thought. It couldn't be. Could it?

I moved it sideways, scared to hope. Then I moved it a bit more. It seemed to be on some kind of hook that you couldn't see. When I moved it as far as it could go, I could see the safe set into the wall.

I nearly screamed with excitement, but stopped myself in time. It would be pretty hard to explain if someone heard me. So I whispered Yes! Yes! Yes! And stood there grinning like an idiot. And then realised I was an idiot. I had found a safe but had no way of getting into it. There was a dial on the front of it but I didn't know what numbers would open it.

I looked around in case a set of numbers appeared, knowing perfectly well that that wasn't how GG did things. I wasn't going to find them in the bathroom cabinet or stuck under the soap dish.

I checked anyway just in case. As I thought, nothing there.

I was stuck. Either a new clue would turn up somewhere or I already had it but wasn't seeing it. I decided to go away and think about it. I locked the door to the flat and took the key back to Mum.

'OK?' she asked.

'Yeah, fine thanks, Mum. Maybe I could go back another time.'

'Yes, of course,' she said. 'Any time.'

I felt a bit guilty about pretending I wanted to be near GG, but that was true really. I did. It just wasn't the whole truth, as he would have said.

I went into the living room. Kelly was watching TV. She ignored me at first, then looked up and said,

'What were you doing in GG's flat?'

'Just being there,' I said. 'Anyway, it's none of your business.'

'Did you find anything?'

That stopped me. 'What do you mean?'

'Which bit of 'Did you find anything?' do you not understand, brother dear?'

'I don't know what you're talking about. I went to GG's flat because I miss him and I wanted to feel near him. Maybe you wouldn't be able to understand someone having feelings.'

She looked a bit shocked at that. 'Sorry, Russ,' she said. 'I didn't mean anything.'

I shrugged and went up to my room. Did a bit of homework. Messed about. Tried not to think about GG and the safe. We had chicken sandwiches, home-made soup and Mum's apple pie for lunch. It was great but my mind wasn't on it. Mum looked disappointed when I just munched my way through it all.

In the afternoon I was playing tennis with Susie. I got changed and went to meet her at the local court. It was the first time I almost wished I wasn't doing it. My mind was so distracted and I had feelings of Ned lurking and maybe Kelly and Susie betraying me to him. Yeah, I know, paranoya again.

Susie was all smiles and chat. She rabbited on about everything except what was on both our minds. No mention of GG's clues, libraries, nasty cousins. I just kept nodding and shaking my head and smiling.

'Hey,' she said, 'where are you? You haven't said a word.'

'Sorry,' I said. 'A bit distracted.'

'Anything new?'

'No, nothing at all.'

I kept thinking of Ned at the library talking to Mr Stewart and hoped it didn't mean anything and that Susie didn't know about it.

We played three sets. Susie beat me two to one which wasn't bad, the way I was feeling. I walked home with her, but said I had stuff to do when she invited me in.

The rest of the day wore on. Dinner, a bit more homework and, eventually, bed. I read for a while, then fell asleep. And began a night of dreams.

It started with a big green field. There were people playing bowls, but the balls were different colours and they kept falling into holes.

Then I heard GG say, 'Good shot.' I was sitting beside him in his living room. We were watching his big telly on the wall. Then I realised the field was a snooker table. It was Ronnie O'Sullivan playing and he was potting reds and blacks. The crowd was getting excited and the commentator said, 'He's going for a maximum.' After he'd potted all the reds and blacks, Ronnie potted all the colours – yellow, green, brown, blue, pink and then the final black. The crowd was going mad and GG was banging the arm of the sofa.

'Brilliant,' he said. 'Ronnie's got another maximum.' And then I woke up. Mr Froyd had done it again.

MAXIMUM!

A maximum in snooker was the highest score you could make. GG loved snooker and I often watched it with him. I knew all the big players and the scores for the different balls. But best of all, I knew what you scored for a maximum.

ONE FOUR SEVEN

That was it. The code for the safe was one four seven.

It had to be.

Hadn't it?

I told myself to calm down. As GG would say *It was all theory*. Until I actually tried it, I wouldn't know whether it was true or not.

The first problem was, if I asked Mum

if I could go back into the flat today, she'd wonder what I was up to. I couldn't say I wanted to be close to GG two days in a row.

The second problem? What if the snooker maximum had nothing to do with it? Well, first things first, as GG would say.

After breakfast, I stayed back and helped Mum load the dishwasher. When it was done, I said, 'Mum, I think I left some homework stuff in GG's flat. I had some notes in my pocket and I was looking at them while I was there.'

'You want the key then?'

'If you wouldn't mind. I can get them myself.'

She handed me the key and I tried to walk calmly out of the kitchen and down the hall. I did sneak a bit of a skip when I was out of sight.

When I got in, there was no time to mess around. I went straight to the bathroom and shoved the cabinet to one side.

A part of me wondered whether I had dreamt the whole thing, so I was relieved when the safe was still there.

OK, crunch time. I pressed one, then

four, then seven. Held my breath and turned the handle. A click and a pull and the door was open.

I pulled out the envelope and ripped it open. There was a folded piece of notepaper like people used to write letters on. I opened it out.

The sight of GG's writing nearly made me cry.

This is to authorise the bearer to have access and retrieve the contents of safe deposit box number 326.

Signed
James Fitzpatrick

My heart was thumping. I was there. The end of the search. Or was it? Was I going to find GG's pocket watch at long last? I couldn't believe it. But I was getting ahead of myself. I hadn't actually got it.

Kelly barged into my room without knocking and I shoved the paper under my pillow.

'What do you want, Miss Politeness?' I

asked

'Look, Russ, don't be like that,' she said. 'I'm trying to help you.'

'And what makes you think I need your help, Miss Smarty?'

I thought she was going to cry. I wasn't usually so horrible to my sister. I just didn't want her messing with my head when everything was beginning to work out.

'Well, that's OK, Mr...uh...Smarty yourself.' Her voice was shaking and she had trouble getting the words out. She ran out of the room and slammed the door. I could hear her crying as she went down the hall. I should have gone after her, but I didn't. And I ended up making life a whole lot harder for myself.

In the meantime, I had to get on with the day-to-day things like school and the family. And I had to think about getting GG's package. I had never been in a bank and wasn't sure what you did. And would they pay any attention to a kid? It was different in the post office. GG and the postmaster were friends. We had been going in there together since I was really young. Then I had an idea. I went downstairs. Mum and Dad were watching the early news on TV.

'Dad,' I said, 'will you be going to the bank anytime soon?'

He gave me a look, sort of grinning and frowning at the same time. 'Why, Russ? Do you want some money?'

'No, it's just this project we have for school. We have to find out about the bank and the post office. It's called learning about life.' I couldn't believe I was getting so good at lying. Would GG have wanted that? I remember him saying 'The end doesn't justify the means.'

When I asked him what it meant, he said you couldn't do something wrong to achieve something good. Where did that leave me? Did little white lies really matter? I didn't know and there was nobody I could ask. Well, I could ask Susie what she thought.

'How about Friday after school?' It was Dad talking. I'd forgotten what I'd asked him. Oh, the bank, of course. Silly me.

'That would be great, Dad. Thanks.' My Dad was an accountant. He would definitely want me to know about banks. And he usually left the office early on Fridays.

'I'll pick you up from school. We can go then.'

I met Susie the next morning.

'I want to ask you something,' I said.

'Ask away.' She gave a little bow.

'It's a bit complicated. How about meeting me after school?'

'OK. See you then.'

It was a great afternoon. The sun was really hot. I took my jacket off while I waited for Susie. A magpie was hopping about the playground. One for sorrow, two for joy. Send me another, I thought. As Susie came out of school, another one flew down from the old oak tree.
Susie came out looking thoughtful. I waved to her. I thought she hadn't seen me at first, but then she walked over to me.

'Hi, there,' I said.

She smiled but her mind seemed far away.

'Look at the magpies,' I said. 'Two of them.'

She looked away. 'What did you want to see me about?'

'What do you think?'

'Not the GG thing?' She was joking but there was something in her voice that wasn't funny.

''Fraid so.' I looked at her. 'What's wrong?'

'Nothing,' she said. 'I'm just tired.'

She sounded like my Mum. People of our age didn't get tired. And when we did, we didn't admit it.

I was getting fed up with this carry on. 'Well do you want to hear about it or not?'

She looked at me then and smiled. 'Course I do, Russ. I'm sorry.'

'Come on, then. Let's go to my place. We can talk in the garden.'

We walked home slowly and talked about all sorts of things. 'Did you know,' she asked, 'that some dinosaurs had wings?'

'Yeah, everyone knows that. How about guns were invented by Leonardo da Vinci?'

'Who'd want to know that?'

We seemed to be back to normal.

When we got home, Mum offered us fruit juice and brownies. Home-made, of course. We sat at the patio table. The sun was still warm and we smiled at each other, more relaxed than we had been for a while.

'This is nice,' she said. 'Sorry, I was

grumpy. Sometimes things aren't so simple.'

'Who are you telling?'

She put her glass down. 'OK, tell me about it.'

I picked up my school bag and got out GG's envelope.

'Look at this,' I said, handing it to her.

She studied the front of the envelope and then opened it. When she took out the paper, her eyes opened wider. 'Wow,' she said.

'Well, what do you think?'

'I think,' she said slowly, 'that you're going to be a lucky person. You'd only put something valuable in a bank, wouldn't you? Have you any idea what it is?'

Crunch time. What GG used to call crossing the Rubicon. I trusted Susie, didn't I? I wasn't sure about her for a very short time, but I felt bad about that. I really trusted her.

'I think it's GG's pocket watch.'

I waited for her reaction of amazement, but she just sat there looking at me.

'Er...,' she said finally. Then she seemed to get it. 'Oh....right, is that what it's all about?'

I wasn't sure what she meant, but I nodded.

'So what are you going to do?' She was very zoned in all of a sudden.

'I've asked Dad to go to the bank with me, just to find out what to do.'

'Oh,' she said, looking a lot happier, 'that's OK then.'

I couldn't figure it out. Anyway, I was going to say something that wouldn't make her happy.

I blurted it out. 'Susie, what's Ned up to?' 'What d'you mean, Russ?' 'He's following me.'

I could see the shock in her eyes. 'No,' she said, 'Ned would never do that. You're imagining it, Russ.'

'OK, so why is he always there, wherever I go?'

She shrugged. 'Maybe you go to the same places.'

I shook my head. 'It's more than that.'

'Then what do you think it is?'

'Aw, forget it,' I said.

She stood up. 'I have to go, Russ. I've got stacks of homework.' She picked up her schoolbag. 'Good luck with the bank.' And with that she was away.

Chapter 8

When Dad and I went to the bank, I was quite nervous. The banks I'd seen in films were big empty spaces with marble floors and pillars. The people were hidden behind glass bullet-proof barriers. Well not exactly hidden; you could see them, but you couldn't get at them.

Our bank was smaller than that. In a way, it was quite cosy. There were ladies behind glass, but you could get near to them and they looked quite human. Dad went up to one of them and I tagged along behind. He said he had an appointment with the manager. We were asked to take a seat.

They had one of those games for kids with plastic things. I would have liked to have a go, but I was too old for it, so I sat looking round while Dad read a magazine called *Money Talks* which was lying on the table. When they called us, the manager, Mr Hawthorne, came out and shook hands with Dad.

Then Dad introduced us. 'Jim, this is Russ. His school is doing a project on banking and he wants to ask you some questions. I suppose you've been tortured by his classmates.'

Jim looked a bit puzzled, but said he was more than happy to tell me anything I wanted to know. I just hoped he wouldn't say that I was the only one who'd asked.

'Well,' I said, 'one thing I'm interested in is where you keep valuable things.'

'Ah,' he said, 'you mean the vault. Well, unfortunately, we can't actually show it you.' He made a face. 'Security. Sorry, Russ.'

I thought quickly. 'Well, how do people get things out, Mr Hawthorne?'

'Ah,' he said slowly. Then he seemed to make his mind up.

'Follow me and I'll show you what happens.' He led us through a door into the private part of the bank. It was a big room with people working at computer stations. He took us into a smaller room with a desk and a few chairs. Then he asked a man called Steve to bring us an empty safe deposit box.

'Ok,' he said. 'This is how it works. A

customer brings in something valuable. They can hire a safe deposit box which has its own key. If they want to take something out, we bring the box out of the vault for them. Or they can just leave something in an envelope which we put in the vault. We give a receipt and the customer needs that and their ID to get their property out.'

My mind was spinning trying to figure out how I could get GG's stuff. I was still afraid to think of it as the pocket watch. When we left the bank, I thought I saw Ned on the other side of the road. I couldn't be sure because the road was busy and he ducked into a shop as soon as we came out.

'Hey, Dad,' I grabbed his arm, 'did you see Ned?'

He looked around and shook his head. 'No, I don't think so. Why?'

I couldn't think of anything to say. I wasn't going to tell him the whole thing now that I was so near to the end.

'Anyway,' he said, 'why wouldn't you see him here? He wouldn't be surprised to see us, would he? I mean, we're on a street in the town where we all live.'

I wasn't so sure about that. I thought

Ned would be very interested to see me and Dad coming out of the bank.

But why did I think that? That was when I really started to think about Ned. GG would have said if you have a problem, look at it, get it clear in your mind. Did I have a problem?

Ned knew that GG had left clues, that I was following a trail. How did he know? Susie said he was there when we were talking about it. I didn't remember that, but I trusted her. Why would she tell Ned about it when I had asked her not to? And why would Ned be interested?

That was the first time I had asked myself that. I was a kid. Ned was an adult. Why would he care about some silly game that my great-grandfather had left for me? Even if he knew about the pocket watch, what difference would it make to him? For the first time, I felt scared. I had been going along on an adventure hoping at the end I would be able to help my family. Was there something more serious going on?

Dad talked about the bank as we were driving home. I think he was trying to tell me everything he knew about banks. It would have been great if I had really wanted to know all that stuff. Then he suggested giving a talk to the class about banking and finance.

'Uh, no thanks, Dad. It's very good of you, but I'd be really embarrassed.'

'OK.' He never made a fuss about stuff like that so I could always be honest with him. Then I remembered that I had lied to him more over the past few weeks than I had in my whole life.

After we got home, I sat in the living room playing my Nintendo. I wasn't really supposed to before homework, but sometimes Mum turned a blind eye as GG would say.

Kelly came in and flopped beside me on the sofa. 'Well,' she said, 'what are you up to?'

I gave her a look and went back to the game.

She looked back. 'Yes, brother dear, I know you're playing your Nintendo. I meant what are you doing in life.'

I ignored her.

She threw a cushion at me. 'Well, what about this GG thing? Have you solved it yet?'

That got my attention. 'What do you mean?'

'You know what I mean. You looked behind the picture and got a message. Then you looked in the old fountain and got the crossword. Then you went to the post office and got a letter. Then you went to GG's flat and then you went to the library. Then you went to the bank with Dad. And I know the school isn't doing a course on banking.'

I didn't know what to make of it. The whole thing seemed to be shaping up into something that was no longer fun. Things were bad with Kelly; not that there was anything new there. Susie was behaving oddly. Ned was lurking about, turning up in suspicious circumstances. And I still hadn't got to the end of the trail. Maybe I should just tell Mum and Dad and let them deal with it. I thought about it but I couldn't do it. Not yet.

I turned to my sister. 'Kelly, for once in your miserable life, will you do something for me?'

'Well, when you put it like that...'

'Sorry,' I said, 'I didn't mean it like that.'

'Oh, yeah, how did you mean it then?'

I was struggling. 'Can we start again?'

She just looked at me.

'I've got something going on. I don't want to talk about it yet. All I can say is, it could be really good for all of us if it works out.'

'You think you're so smart,' she said. 'Well, you don't know everything.' She got up and walked out.

I shrugged and went up to my room. I had hidden GG's envelope under my pillow. I did my homework and then took it out and read the words over and over. This entitles the bearer, etc etc. I held it against me, looking round to make sure no one was watching. I still wasn't sure it was the watch, but if it was, when would I be able to get it out of the bank?

The next morning, I met Susie on the way to school.

'Well?' she asked.

'Well what?'

'You know. Did you go to the bank?'

'I did.'

'And did you learn anything?'

'I learned a whole lot of stuff. How bank vaults work, where it is, how you get something out of it. I had to stop my Dad from coming to school to give a lecture.'

She laughed. 'You're becoming a

brilliant liar.'

'Don't say that.' I shook my head. 'I hate lying. When this is over, I'm never going to tell another lie.'

'Look,' she said, 'sometimes you have to, so you might as well be good at it.'

Wise words, I suppose. Sometimes Susie was a lot wiser than I was. Girls were like that, even though we didn't give them credit for it.

'So you're at the end of the line?'

'Yeah.'

She came near to me and put her hand on mine. 'Good luck,' she said.

I could have hugged her. 'Thanks,' I said.

As I left her and started up the road to home, I saw Ned out of the corner of my eye. He didn't seem to be going anywhere in particular; I couldn't actually say he was following me. When I got to the gate, I looked round, but he was gone.

I was going to have to get my act together and do it. I was scared and nervous and uncertain and hopeful and so many things, I couldn't get my head round it. All I had to do was go to the bank, give them the letter, take the package and that would be it. So what was stopping me? Well, I was scared and nervous and.....all that. And I wasn't sure whether they would give it to me.

Maybe you had to be eighteen or something.

And there was Ned. Why was I scared of Ned? What could he do? I couldn't get him out of my head. I kept seeing him, his skinny figure, his little beard and dark hair, his stary eyes that seemed to look through you.

There was something threatening about him even when he was being friendly. Why was he following me? He couldn't know what was in the bank vault. Even I didn't know. I just hoped it was GG's pocket watch.

I told Mum and Dad I was meeting Susie for a game of tennis.

'See you,' I said to Kelly. She just looked bored.

As I headed towards the bank, I could feel the envelope in my pocket. I held it tightly, rubbing my thumb against it. GG I thought please let this be it.

I was getting so used to seeing Ned behind me every time I went out, that I looked round to make sure he was there.

Then I thought What's wrong with you, man?

Anyway, he wasn't there so it didn't matter. I was free of him and it felt great. I strolled along towards the bank, whistling.

How dumb can you be? As I turned the corner on Westbury Street, he was there.

'Hi, Russ,' he said, 'going somewhere?'

'Nowhere in particular.' I shrugged. There was no way I was going any further.

'What have you got in your pocket?' he asked.

I looked down realising that the bit of the envelope with the bank logo was sticking out.

'Nothing,' I said, trying to push it in.

'Let's see then.' He reached out towards me and I jumped back.

'Get off,' I shouted and turned and ran. I could hear him laughing as I took off up the street. I forgot all about playing tennis and arrived home panting.

'That was quick.' Dad was in the kitchen, fiddling with some dish he was making.

I just remembered in time. 'Susie

wasn't feeling well,' I said. 'We had to cancel.'

'Oh, that's a shame.' He looked at me and I wondered whether too many odd things had happened. And whether I was getting in over my head.

'Uh, Dad,' I said.

'Mm?'

But I wasn't ready yet. I said, 'Nothing.'

He went back to his work and I drifted into the living room.

Kelly was watching TV with her feet up on the sofa. 'Shouldn't you be getting more exercise?' I asked.

She yawned loudly and raised her fingers.

Mum and Dad certainly weren't doing a great job with her.

I still hadn't worked out what to do. If Ned was going to follow me every time I went out, I was going to have to figure out some way of putting him off. I couldn't think of anything so I went upstairs and did my homework.

The next morning in maths class I had an idea. Some of the boys walked past the bank on the way home. If I went with them, Ned wouldn't notice me if he was watching. I caught them in the locker room before we left for the day.

'I have to get a leaflet from the bank for my Mum,' I said. 'Can I walk up with you guys?'

'Sure, Russ.' Charlie Burns had been at my birthday party. 'Are you ready to go?'

'Yep.' I got into the middle of them and kept my head down. When we got to the bank, I had a quick look round. No sign of Ned.

I tried to look as if I knew what I was doing when I went up to the counter. The lady cashier smiled at me in that superior way adults have.

'Can I help you?' she asked.

'Uh, I was here the other day about the bank vault.'

'I remember you,' she said.

'Well, I have a letter from my great-grandfather saying I can collect a packet from the vault.'

She took GG's envelope and looked at it. 'I'll have to ask the manager. Would you like to wait over there.'

I sat by the kid's game trying to look cool. After a few minutes, Mr Hawthorne came out of his office and walked over.

'Russ,' he said and shook my hand.

'What can I do for you?'

I explained about GG and the instructions. 'Ah, yes,' he said. 'I understand. The problem is, Russ, that your great-grandfather is no long with us. Anything he left would have to go into his estate. I think your Dad is his executor. I could give whatever is held in the vault to him.' He handed me back the letter.

'Right,' I said, 'thanks, Mr Hawthorne. I'll ask my Dad to call in.' I ran home without looking around. I wasn't sure what to do next. Tell Dad the whole story and let him take over? I wouldn't have to worry about Ned if I did that. But I didn't want to. I really didn't want to. This was between me and GG and I wanted to finish it.

I told Susie about it. 'So I don't know what's in the bank. And I can't get it without asking Dad.'

'I don't see what else you can do, Russ. Otherwise you'd have to give up the whole thing.'

'I know, but I'd feel as if I was giving it up anyway.'

She smiled. 'You always want to do everything for yourself, don't you?'

'Do I?' I didn't think of myself that way. I felt pretty pathetic at the moment. 'And I don't know how to tell Dad. If I tell him everything, he's going to ask why I didn't tell him before. But I can't think of any way of asking him to get whatever it is out of the bank.'

'Well, why don't you go back to the beginning? Say you found a note in the roof space which told you about the bank. You wanted to do it yourself, but the bank won't give it to you.'

I nodded. 'I could try it I suppose. Thanks, Susie.'

'No problem. Let me know how you get on.'

Chapter 9

I had to wait until Dad got home from work. He was a bit grumpy and I didn't want to annoy him. Mum put the dinner out and we sat eating without talking. It felt awkward.

Usually we all talked our heads off. Kelly started rabbiting on about some stupid thing that had happened to her at school.

'And I just hate Jeannie Quinn,' she said.

'She knew I wanted to be the princess and she chose Millie Young.' Mum gave her a look and she shut up. I wondered what was going on. After dinner, Mum was loading the dishwasher. Kelly escaped pretty fast. I wondered how she would ever learn to be a woman, never mind a princess. Dad seemed to be hovering around. He kept looking at me until I took the hint and went out of the kitchen. I stood in the hall for a minute, thinking about how to tackle the bank problem.

'It's not looking good.' Dad was talking.

'Has something happened?' Mum sounded worried so I stayed listening.

'They've let Owen go.'

Owen was a junior in Dad's office.

'That's a shame. What will he do?' Mum sounded as if she really cared.

'I don't know. But the worry is once they start letting people go, we're all in danger.'

'But surely not you. How would they manage without you?'

Dad laughed. 'Nice of you to say so. I don't know whether they'd see it the same way.'

There was silence for a while. Mum had stopped loading the dishwasher while she was talking to Dad. Then she started again. All I could hear was the rattle of cutlery.

When she stopped there was silence again. Then she said, 'If things did go wrong, how bad would it be?'

I could hear Dad lighting a cigarette. He never smoked in the house.

'They might cut me down to half time. Which means half the money.'

'Which means we wouldn't be able to

afford the mortgage?' It sounded like a question, but it was obvious she knew the answer.

I could sense him nodding. 'We could lose the house.'

I went upstairs. I still had to figure out how to get Dad to go to the bank. When I got to my room, I glanced out of the window. What I saw made my heart jump. Kelly was standing at the front gate with Ned. I stood there watching, wondering what they were talking about. Ned leaned towards her and seemed to be whispering in her ear. Kelly started laughing and poked him in the chest. I wanted to rush down and drag her into the house.

I thought about opening the window and shouting, 'Kelly, what are you doing?' I kept saying it to myself, over and over. Then Ned looked up. For a horrible moment we stared at each other. He turned away first. Then he said something to Kelly before walking off down the street.

I ran down the stairs and met her as she came in through the front door. 'What were you doing with Ned?' I shouted.

She gave me a look and walked past

me up the hall. I grabbed her arm.

'Kelly,' I said, 'what were you talking to Ned about?' My voice was shaking with fear and anger.

'Brother, dear,' she said, 'is it really any of your business?'

'Kelly,' I gave her a little shake, 'you don't know what you're doing. He's evil.'

She pulled away from me. 'Don't be silly. He's nice. I really like him.' She made a face at me. 'And there's nothing you can do about it.'

I couldn't say anything to Dad when he and Mum were so worried. I shouted goodnight to them and went to bed.

The next morning, Dad and I were first down to breakfast. He got cereal for me and coffee for himself.

'Dad,' I said, when we were sitting at the table, 'there's something I want to ask you.'

'What's that, Russ?' He took a sip of coffee.

I had thought carefully about what to say.

'GG left me a message. I found it in the roof space among his things.'

First he didn't seem to hear me, then he looked shocked as if the words had just gone in.

'Why didn't you tell us?'

'Well, it was between me and GG. I wanted to find out what it was about first.'

'Oh.' He was still frowning.

'I'm sorry, Dad. I didn't think you'd mind.'

'Well, it's not that I mind. It's just a bit hurtful. I miss him, too, you know.'

I felt rotten. But I still couldn't tell him the whole story. Call me stubborn, but this was between me and GG. 'I know, Dad. I really am sorry.'

He smiled. 'It's OK, Russ. Anyway, what did you want to ask me?'

'Well, there seems to be something in the bank for me.'

He looked really shocked at that. 'What do you mean something in the bank? GG didn't have a bank account. He used the post office for everything.'

This was tricky. 'I think it was a sort of joke. You know the way he used to leave messages and trails for me when he was... here.'

He nodded. 'But if there was anything in the bank, it should have gone into his estate.'

'It's probably only a message,' I said.

'OK, we can go tomorrow. I'm working late tonight.'

'Thanks, Dad.'

It was a long day at school. I was getting to the end of GG's trail. Somehow I felt close to him. I kept seeing different pictures in my head of his kindly old face: his smile when I beat him at Scrabble, his frown when he was trying to work out a puzzle, his grin when I made a joke.

Was he watching me from somewhere outside our universe? Would I find his pocket watch at the end of the journey? I missed him so much. Did he miss me? Or was he still with me in some way that I didn't know?

Then there was the problem of Kelly and Ned. What were they up to? Would my little sister betray me? Could she? She didn't really know anything about my search. Or did she? She seemed to sneak up on me at odd times. Was she telling my secrets to Ned?

I met Susie after school and felt happy for the first time in days. 'Hi,' I said.

'Hi, yourself. What's new?'

'Don't ask.'

'That bad?'

'I don't know. It seems that way.'

'So tell me about it.'

I didn't know where to start. 'It's this GG thing,' I said.

'No kidding?'

'OK, there's never anything else these days.'

'What's the latest, then?'

I told her about the bank and Dad and how I hoped this was the end of it.

'I thought you were enjoying it. The puzzles are fun, aren't they?'

'Yeah.'

'You don't sound convinced.'

I didn't want to tell her again about Ned following me. I wasn't even sure he was.

And if I told her about him talking to Kelly, she'd think I was losing it. He was her cousin. Why shouldn't he talk to my sister?

'So when are you going to the bank with your Dad?' she asked when we reached the end of her road.

'Tomorrow, I think.'

She nodded and said 'Bye.'

I raised a hand.

When I got home, Dad was there. 'Change of plans,' he said. 'I'm working late tomorrow instead of today.'

'Great,' I said, thinking that if Susie was telling Ned what I was doing, she'd get it wrong this time. Then I felt ashamed. Susie wouldn't betray me.

'So, let's go.'

We drove to the bank and Dad found a parking space opposite. When we went in, he asked for the manager. I was watching through the window for Ned and I missed what was going on. I knew they were talking and Dad showed him papers. After that the manager went away. When he came back, he handed Dad an envelope.

That was when I realised Dad's hands were shaking. I looked at his face and I could see that he was really excited.

'What's in it, Dad?' I asked, feeling pretty excited myself.

'What?' He had forgotten I was there. He turned away as he opened the envelope. I could see my name printed on it in GG's writing. Dad pulled a paper out and read it.

He made a noise like he was disgusted and shoved the paper over at me.

'Here,' he said, 'it's a load of rubbish.'

I took it and read the words slowly.

The message is the key. The key is the

message. Ave atque vale.

I looked up at Dad and shrugged.

'What does ave atque vale mean?' I asked, just for something to say. I knew perfectly well what it meant. It was GG's final message.

'It's one of those old Latin expressions. It means hail and farewell.'

'Oh.'

'Let's go,' he said.

We drove home in silence each thinking our thoughts.

That night when I went to bed, I said,'OK, Mr Froyd. If ever I needed you, I need you now.' I was asleep in five minutes.

The next day I didn't have time to think about GG's message. It was go all day with a maths test, computer time and the finals of an inter-school soccer match. After school, I took off my PE gear and met Susie in the playground.

'Well?' she asked.

'Do you know,' I said, 'that's what you say to me every time we meet. It's getting boring.'

She gave me a look. 'Don't bother telling me then.'

'Sorry.' How is it that girls always put you on the back foot? 'We went to the bank. I got an envelope. There was a message inside. It said the message was the key.'

'What does that mean?'

'I don't know. Dad was disgusted. I think he hoped it was going to be the answer to all his troubles.'

'What troubles?'

I could have kicked myself. 'Nothing,' I said. 'Just an expression.'

We just talked about school stuff after that. But I was beginning to get a glimmer of something.

After I left Susie at the end of her road, I ran the rest of the way home. When I got there, Mum grabbed me and started giving off about the state of my room.

'It's OK,' I said. 'That's the way I like it.'

'Well, I don't. So go up there and tidy it.'

Great timing, Mum, I thought. By the time I had the room done, dinner was ready and I had to wait another half hour before I could think about GG's message.

After dinner, I went up to my room

to think. I thought I knew the answer. It was the key that was the key, if you know what I mean. At least I thought it was. I had remembered GG's box of keys. The problem was Mum and Dad had cleared GG's flat after he went to heaven and I hadn't a clue whether the keys were still there.

I had to wait till the next morning. I came down early and sneaked into GG's flat before the rest of them were around. Where to start? I knew the key box was in a cupboard, but I couldn't remember which one. I checked all the kitchen cupboards again, even looking in the oven and microwave. Nothing. It wasn't in the bathroom.

I started with the wardrobe in the bedroom. I had to climb on a stool to reach the top. I felt around and suddenly there it was, right at the back in the corner. It was a small metal box with two dolphins carved on the top. For a moment I held it against me. Then I couldn't stop the tears. I just let them come.

After a while, I pulled myself together. I hadn't cried so much since GG had died. But it was time to move on. I opened the box. It was just as I remembered. A bunch of keys all mixed up, some with string, others with rings or chains. Then I spotted a difference.

There was a small key-shaped container lying at the bottom of the tin. I lifted it out. It was made of gold-coloured plastic. There was a crack along one side and a tiny metal button. When I pressed the button, the case opened. There was a metal key with piece of cardboard on a length of thread. GG had written on the card

Weston Station. Locker No 43.

Was it finally the end of the trail? Well, OK not quite the end. I still had to go to the station and open the locker. I was thinking about it when I heard Mum shouting 'Russ. Where are you? It's time for breakfast.'

I'd forgotten about school. How to get back without anyone seeing me? Then I had it. Through the garden. I shoved the key in my pocket and went out through GG's patio doors. When I came in through the kitchen door, Mum said, 'What were you doing out there?'

'Nothing,' I shrugged. 'Just walking

round the garden.'

'Well, eat your breakfast. You're going to be late for school.' She sounded cross.

Chapter 10

I walked up the road. Susie was waiting at the corner.

'Hi,' she said, all cheerful for once.

'Well?' I asked.

She gave me a look, then laughed. 'Very funny.'

I couldn't keep it in any longer. 'I've solved it.'

'What do you mean? The whole thing?'

'Yep. Well, I haven't got whatever it is yet, but I know where it is.'

'Well, are you going to tell me or not?'

I took the key case out of my pocket and opened it. 'There you go.'

She took the key and card and read the message carefully. 'Wow.'

'I know.'

'What do you think it is? Do you really think it's the pocket watch?'

'I don't know. I hope so.'

'When are you going?'

'Probably Saturday. I can't go after school. It would take too long and I'd need a reason.'

'Can I come with you?'

I was tempted. If Ned was there, he wouldn't do anything in front of Susie. Or would he? I didn't want to get Susie involved in something nasty.

'Look,' I said, 'thanks for offering, but I feel I have to do this myself. I'll come up afterwards and show you whatever it is. OK?'

'OK.' She looked disappointed. Then she frowned at me. 'You'll be careful, won't you?'

'Course.' I laughed.

I sounded better than I felt.

On Friday night I went to bed early. I told Mum I was going into town the next morning.

'There's a few things I want to look for,' I said, hoping she wouldn't ask for details but she didn't seem interested.

I couldn't sleep. After a while I got up and started to walk around. I could hear Kelly snoring in her room. I thought of taping her in case she didn't believe me, but I couldn't be bothered. She probably wouldn't believe it was her anyway.

I could hear Mum and Dad talking in the living room. I went down to listen not for any reason, just for something to do.

The next thing, Mum started to cry. I heard Dad get up and walk across the room. 'Look,' he said, 'if the worst comes to the worst, we'll sell the house and rent something. We're not going to be homeless.'

Mum was sobbing. 'I can't bear it. It's not fair. We've worked hard all our lives and now we're going to lose our home. And what about the kids? They'll be devastated. Russ loves this house. And I was going to let him have GG's flat when he's older.'

I had never even thought of that. I would love it. I decided then that I would do whatever I had to. If I could save the house, I would face Ned whatever he threatened and I WOULD WIN.

The next morning, I got up at eight o'clock. Dad was early too and we had breakfast together. We didn't talk much and he kept sighing. After we had cleared the plates, I said, 'Can I go up into the roof space, Dad?'

'I suppose so, son. What do you want to go up for?' He didn't seem all that interested.

'There's a couple of GG's things I want

to look at.'

'Oh,' he said. 'OK, I'll put the ladder up.'

'Thanks, Dad.'

'In fact, there's one or two things I need to get. I'll come up too.'

That was the last thing I wanted. He fixed the ladder and climbed up. I waited until he had gone through the opening, then I followed him. I pretended to be going through GG's books while Dad rummaged about among his own stuff.

When he had got his things, he said,

'Well, are you finished?'

'Not yet,' I said. 'You go on down, Dad. I've still a few more things to look at.'

Thankfully, he started climbing down the ladder. As soon as he was out of sight, I opened the army box. The gun was buried under GG's uniform. I checked that it was unloaded the way GG had shown me. Then I wrapped it in one of his shirts. I picked up a book as cover and went down the ladder.

No one was around, so I went up to my room. The gun was bigger than I remembered. I tried to stuff it in my trouser pocket, but it wouldn't fit. I thought for a minute maybe I should leave it behind. Then I thought of Ned and decided there was no way I was going without it. The question was how to carry it. Then I thought of my rucksack. I got it out of the wardrobe and put the gun in the inside pocket.

I called goodbye to Mum and Dad. Kelly asked why I was carrying a rucksack, but I was ready for that.

'If I buy something, I'm not going round with a plastic bag.'

Kelly made a rude noise and I closed the front door behind me.

Even before I got to the end of the drive, I felt scared. I looked up and down the street, but there was no one there except an old couple walking along arm in arm. I set off towards town, thinking this was the most stupid thing I had ever done. Then I thought of Mum crying and Dad's worried face.

The town had the usual Saturday crowd. Every shop seemed to have a sale on and Main Street was crammed with people on a mission. I fought my way through the worst of it, watching out for any sign of Ned. It eased as I got to the end of the shopping area and I could walk freely.

Half-way to the station, I felt I was being watched. I didn't want to turn round, so I stopped and pretended to tie my shoe. I had a quick look behind me, but no one was there. As I walked on, I had the same feeling. It was as if an electric ray was poking me in the back. I knew it was imagination, but I couldn't stop the feeling.

The station was nearly empty. Everyone was shopping, nobody travelling. I looked around to see where the lockers were. That was when I saw Ned. He ducked behind a pillar, but he wasn't quick enough. This was crunch time. It was Ned or me. And it wasn't just me. If Ned won, my family lost. GG, help me. And he did. I remembered his time in France and the German soldiers. That's where it all began. The French nobleman had given him the pocket watch. I was about to find it. That's where the search was going to end.

And then Ned was there, grinning and waving. 'OK, boy,' he shouted. 'Let's get this finished.'

GG had found a way of putting the soldiers out of commission. But he was lucky. The swimming pool had been there waiting. I could feel him trying to tell me something. Or maybe I just worked it out for myself. There's no point complaining about what you haven't got. You have to use what comes to hand. Was there anything in the station that I could use to keep Ned away from me until I got to the locker?

And I got it. GG had a swimming pool. The railway line was set way below the platform. If I could get Ned into it, it would take him time to get out again. He was facing me and the drop was behind him.

I pulled out GG's gun. Ned's mouth became a big O, his nasty little beard like something stuck on his chin. The shock in his eyes nearly made me laugh, but I never changed my stern expression.

'Back off,' I said.

And he did. Right over the edge of the platform onto the line. Maybe he hurt himself when he fell. Or he was so scared, he stayed down. I ran along the platform past the sign pointing to the lockers.

There was a wall of metal doors, each with its white number on a black disc. I found Number 43 and pushed the key in the lock. It turned easily and I opened the door.

And there it was. GG's pocket watch lying there waiting for me. I picked it out, slammed the locker door, shoved the watch in my pocket and ran to the exit. As I passed the place where Ned had fallen over, I kept back against the wall. There was no sign of him.

I left the station running and didn't slow down until I reached the end of our road. Then I had a quick look back. No Ned. Puffing and panting like a 60-a-day man, I slowed to a walk. When I saw our driveway, I nearly started to cry. Dad was standing outside the front door.

'Ah, there you are,' he said. 'I was beginning to wonder what had happened to you.'

'Oh, nothing,' I said, trying to look cool. Then I couldn't keep it up. 'Dad.' I ran up to him. 'I've got it. GG's pocket watch.' I pulled it out and handed it to him.

I'll never forget his face. First it was blank, like a mask. Then he looked at me and smiled but there were tears in his eyes. 'How did you do it, Russ?'

I thought what fun I would have

telling him and Mum and Kelly over and over, reliving the story, going over the puzzles. And Susie. And then I remembered.

'Ned,' I said. 'He fell onto the railway line. He was following me.'

I nearly mentioned the gun but stopped myself in time. 'What if there's a train?'

Dad looked shocked. I wasn't sure whether it was because of Ned following me or the danger of the train.

'It's OK, son,' he said, 'don't worry, I'll ring the station.' The rest of the day was a blur.

I remembered the gun that night after dinner. The ladder to the roof space was still up and I told Mum and Dad I wanted to go up and be alone for a few minutes with GG's things. They were very understanding about it. I carried the gun up and replaced it in the military box.

I found out later that Ned banged his head on the railway line and was taken to A & E. They checked him out but he was OK. Apparently, he told everyone I had pulled a gun on him. I just laughed and said how silly was that? Everyone put it down to the knock on his head.

There were things I still didn't get. I had to talk to Susie. I couldn't get away from the family until the next morning, so I rang her in the lull before lunch when everyone was in the kitchen.

'Oh, hello, Russ,' she said. She was a bit low.

'Hi, Susie. Can you meet me?'

There was a long pause. Then she said, 'Uh, sure, Russ. What time and where?'

'How about after lunch - at the half-way corner?'

Another pause. 'OK. See you then.'

I hung up and shook my head.

Over lunch, the talk was still all about GG and the pocket watch and Russ's incredible bravery and cleverness and all the things a guy wants to hear.

Then I realised that Kelly hadn't said a word to me since I came back from the station. I decided to catch her later. She still had some explaining to do.

Chapter 11

Susie was wearing jeans and a red shirt. She walked slowly up to the corner, her long fair hair swaying from side to side. As I got nearer to her, I smiled and raised my hand. She just looked back. Then she started to cry.

'Oh, Russ, I'm so sorry.'

'What are you talking about Susie?' I tried to hug her, but she went all stiff and shook me off.

She stood there rubbing her eyes; then she looked straight at me. 'I betrayed you.'

I didn't know what to say.

'I didn't mean to,' she said. 'At first it was just a game with Ned, trying to solve your puzzles. He was really interesting and helpful. I...gave him stuff and then pretended I hadn't. I never meant any harm.'

'I know that Susie.'

'Then he worked out it was probably the pocket watch GG had hidden. I had told him the story before and he said you might be in danger going about on your own, especially if you found it. He said he would follow you to make sure you were OK. So I told him where you were going. Then I got suspicious. He was too eager. Then he asked if I knew how much the watch was worth. I was so happy when your Dad was going to the bank with you.'

She took a breath. 'Next thing Ned lost his job at the garage. They caught him borrowing cars. I didn't tell him any more. I don't know how he knew about the station.'

I was pretty sure I knew: Little Miss Who Couldn't Keep out of My Business.

'It's OK, Susie. You were just trying to help. Anyway, there's no harm done.

Everything's come out all right in the end.' I hugged her again and that time she let me.

When I got home, Kelly was sitting with her feet on the coffee table watching TV.

'I want to talk to you,' I said. 'In my room.'

She nodded and followed without a word. That surprised me. I'd expected to be told where to go.

I closed the door and we sat down, me on the desk chair and Kelly on the bed.

'I'm sorry, Russ,' she said. 'Truly, truly sorry.'

That took the words out of my mouth. 'Oh,' I said and couldn't say another word.

'I didn't know what was going on,' she went on. 'I trusted Ned and you were always so snottery with me, I wanted to get back at you.'

'So you told him what I was doing.'

She nodded. 'He said he was worried about you, that you were getting in out of your depth. He wanted to protect you.'

I thought about this for a minute. 'But how did you know about the station? I didn't tell anyone about that.' Well, I had told Susie but Kelly didn't need to know that.

She went red. 'I saw the ticket.'

'But it was hidden.'

'I know,' she said. 'I'm sorry.'

'But how did you find it?'

'Russ, I know where you hide things – the bottom drawer of your chest, under your pillow or on top of the wardrobe.'

'You searched my room?'

She nodded. 'Look, I've told you I'm sorry and I really am. Can't we start again and be friends?'

It was a nice idea. And I had been a bit superior at times.

'Course we can,' I said. We hugged each other and then jumped back and laughed, embarrassed.

GG's pocket watch turned out to be worth £100,000. Dad was able to pay off the mortgage. From the money left over, he got the fountain restored for Mum. The soil was cleared from around it and the stonework cleaned. It was surrounded by a circle of special stones which matched it.

Dad put a red rose at its base. We had a grand opening in the garden and they let me invite Susie.

Dad opened a bottle of champagne for himself and Mum. Susie, Kelly and I had fizzy drinks. When our glasses were filled, Dad switched on the water. It rose up in a shower which sparkled like the champagne.

Dad raised his glass and said,

'Here's to Russ.'

After we drank, no one said anything. Then we all raised our glasses together.

'To GG,' we said.

Still not sleepy?

Can you complete the crossword faster than Russ ? No cheating now !!

ACROSS

How many more without feeling? (6)
. Were you in stitches? Sounds like it (2)
. Not against? (4)
. An endless fart? (3)
. Beginning to doubt (2)
. Could be better (4)
2. Had his chips? (3)
3. Prehistoric mammal. Spell it. (2)
4. An article heads south east (5)
5. What a snail delivers? (4)

DOWN

1. Love of tennis (7)
2. Container for a dumb ox? (3)
4. Does the poet put them before worth?
6. In the midst of actors? (2)
9. Skater in the ditch? (6)
10. H-hail? (4)
11. Germany says no (4)
14. Some tool (3)
15. Scatter seed endlessly (2)